CATHEDRAL

CRADLE OF DARKNESS, BOOK ONE

ADDISON CAIN

©2019 by Addison Cain
All rights reserved.

No part of the book may be reproduced or transmitted in any form or by any means, electronic or mechanical, including photocopying, recording, or by any information storage and retrieval system, without permission in writing from the author.

This is a work of fiction. Names, characters, businesses, places, events and incidents are either the products of the author's imagination or used in a fictitious manner. Any resemblance to actual persons, living or dead, or actual events is purely coincidental.

Cover art by Dark City Designs

1

JADE

I have a taste for fine red wine.

Elusive, decadent. It pours down one's throat with all the richness of desire. It can even be thick on the tongue. But it's nothing to the drenched, pervasive cream that smeared over my lips.

Blue-blooded and smug as smog, Ethan knew this as he stood beside my bed, stroking his cock while I hummed appreciation at my surprise.

He wanted me to taste him... dripping from another.

And that's how I found myself awoken from slumber. The smoothly waxed lower lips of a pretty female, caressing my smile.

The slip and glide as she performed exactly as Ethan must have instructed, teased me to take a lick.

Labia puffy from a recent fucking, the tang of female lubrication churned creamy by male ejaculate.

She smelled like life that I was only too happy to let pour down my throat.

Opening my mouth, I dragged the flat of my tongue through the mess. Hooking it so I might catch his cum all in a glob for Ethan's unwavering stare to absorb as he rubbed new life into his recently spent cock.

Salty, an exclusively human bleach-like tang. I knew his taste well.

One might consider me a sexual deviant, the way I rolled his flavor around on my tongue. How I swallowed before grabbing the globes of the offered treat's ass to move her where I would.

Though she enjoyed my exuberance, this act was not about her gratification. It was about mine. Twisting my tongue through her folds as her legs shook from the pleasure, seeking flavor and lingering juices, I devoured.

As if I never need come up for air.

I didn't.

I could hold my breath for hours. Days even.

Which gave me all the time in the world to dig my tongue into her cunt and scoop out the remainder of my prize. Her toned ass, clenched in my hands, bore the sharper edges of my nails, as I took so much more than I gave.

Even so, even though the sensation was too much, rubbing her clit on my nose, she came.

The noises, the squeaks and squawks, *the honesty of them*, excited me.

So I spread my thighs so Ethan might see.

Thinking he was king of the world, he climbed between them, his heartbeat fast and loud. "God, Jade, you two are fucking hot together!"

It must have been near noon, for I could feel the sun cut through the floor to ceiling windows my penthouse afforded, overlooking the city's most exclusive view. The weight of that direct light danced on my pale skin, the unseen pain I was an expert at concealing bleeding together with the impatient stab of a cockhead through my slit.

I sleeved him, wrapped around his turgid length, and bore down in a way the delicious snack riding my face never could. He fought me to remain seated, jerking his meat through the clamp of a satin-coated cunt.

Knees braced to black silk, a bruising grip on my splayed thighs, I didn't need to see him to know the vision before me. Sweat dampening his blond hair, leaving it to hang in his eyes as his lips parted in a blissed-out groan, Ethan strained. He strained to fuck a hole so tight I'd forced him out before his balls might slap my ass.

"God damn..." Equal parts frustration and awe, he bullied his way back inside. Half-seated, he landed a slap on my clit as if to punish the teasing cunt he did so love to conquer. The sting did its work. My muscles jumped just enough that he gained an inch.

The throaty noise of victory made me smile against the woman too sensitive and no longer interested in my mouth. Not that she would *ever* say so aloud. Whoever might have the fun of playing third to our duet knew that they had a body, and it was here for our use.

Complain, and be easily replaced by the next pretty blonde who caught Ethan's eye.

So she tolerated my nips and licks, how I gasped against her when my lover's thumbs pulled the pretty hood of skin away from my clitoris. Threatening me with excessive pleasure, Ethan hissed, "Let me in, Jade."

I softened just enough for him to sink another inch, rippling around his girth in an ancient tease.

The pad of his pointer finger rubbed my exposed clit with the perfect pressure to trick my body into surrender. Just like that, straining and bucking, manic hips between creamy thighs, I was fucked for breakfast.

When I'd tossed the girl away, forgetting she panted at my side while I made frenzied love to Ethan, I couldn't say. One moment we played with her, the next we did not.

Because it was never about whoever else we brought into our bed. They were a garnish, unmemorable.

That wasn't because we were cruel. Ethan for all his failings, was a nice guy. I, despite my heritage, never hurt them.

"I love you, Jade." Delivered with perfect timing, Ethan, believing his proclamation was true, got what he wanted.

Eye's rolling back, his cock expanding with imminent release, my lover enjoyed his second orgasm of the day. One my own climax drove past the pale as my internal muscles twisted tight, released, cramped, and fought to expel him.

"Oh my god! *Oh my god*!" Face the very image of ruin, Ethan threw back his head. The following animal whine, the way he swayed as if on the brink of a faint, it led me to be merciful.

Again I opened, the seed I'd choked off from bursting down its tube allowed to splash against my womb.

Falling to his hands, forehead to mine, he panted through the following waves of euphoria, while I cooed in his ear and ran a comforting caress down his spine.

"I fucking love you, Jade."

Melting into the mattress, my mind wandered through ecstasy and pain. The sun had climbed higher; soon I'd be forced to move. But for now, the hidden cameras needed to see.

I had done my duty for the day.

Though it was permitted, there was no expectation that I come. My orders were only to be seeded.

Daily.

Which made it doubly lovely that I had gotten this reproductive requirement out of the way so early in my schedule. Perhaps I'd even partake again later instead of leaving Ethan to play with his latest toy, should the mood strike him to get his dick wet.

Warm weight of toned male flesh sliding off my body, Ethan stood with a sheepish smile. After taking my fingers to kiss with adoration, he sauntered off to the bathroom to shower.

Eventually his father would require him to show up at corporate HQ and make an official appearance. Dashing smile, suit immaculate, and model beautiful, he'd be expected to do nothing more than saunter in and fuck around at his computer for an hour or two. I imagine he spent it playing Candy Crush or dallying with the prettier girls in the building.

Entitlement at its polished finest. That was my darling Ethan Parker.

"I'm going to join him." Despite the aneurism-inducing orgasm I'd given her, it seemed the girl at my side had collected herself. Standing on shapely tan legs, she meandered towards the ensuite's steaming shower and the man whistling inside it.

Arms stretched overhead, I enjoyed the zippering pops of my spine. "You do that."

Throwing me a smile over her shoulder, she blew me a kiss.

What was her name? Polly?

Vaguely remembering some *Polly wants a cracker* reference, I couldn't recall if this blonde was Polly or if the last blonde had been Polly. Jenny?

Sam?

No, not Sam. Sam had been the curly-haired Venus from last winter.

They all ran together. They all giggled the same, pouted the same, and sported the large gravity defying breasts Ethan had an eye for.

God bless the surgeons who gave those pretty, carefree girls such perfect tits...

For God sure as fuck never blessed me.

And I'm not talking about breasts. My breasts were lovely.

I was stunning, in fact. Dark hair, porcelain skin, designed to draw adoration and attention.

Wealth? I had more money than any man could spend in a lifetime.

But I was not favored by God, and never would be.

After all, I was the child of Lucifer.

2

Perfume.

    The scent of good taste and deep pockets. Specially blended to my precise specifications.

Over the multitude of years, only one distinctive blend has graced my throat. The ritual of application, the slip of cut crystal chilling a scented trail down my skin—I found it comforting, even if I have never enjoyed the smell.

With the inevitable passage of time, everything changes. Trends, styles, freedoms... but this concoction, the way it alters the air around me, *what it signifies*, is as ageless as I am.

In the modern, more sophisticated era, several of the ingredients sloshing within the crystal vial gracing my vanity were extremely illegal. Some so rare, their acquisition cost a greater sum than the annual rent on our metropolis' finest penthouses. Humans of a certain cut, whether it was ingrained in them from high birth, or because they conquered the upper echelon and elbowed their way in, need only take a sniff to know precisely what the cloud of scent signifies.

Affluence. Reverence.

Souls feel me linger in the air long after I've left a room.

Their brains tickled and twitched over a ghost of memory they can't pin down.

As if they'd known me all their lives.

They have. They just can't remember.

"Uncle Randal wants to know if your father will be joining us at his birthday soirée tonight." Attention locked on his phone, Ethan scrolled through his messages, as if what he asked were nothing.

I stopped humming.

No breath entered my lungs; my heart shuddered to a stop. Still as a corpse, no longer musing over frivolous perfume, my eyes rose in the mirror, waiting for Ethan to glance away from his phone.

I cannot imagine what he saw on my face, but I knew it was not the shattered glass panic scratching at my veins.

To him, that flippant remark and the assumption behind it were... innocent.

To me, it felt as if the room was a dead thing rising from the grave.

Speak of the devil and he will appear.

Though Ethan was about as deep as a puddle, even he took note of my brief lapse from flawless composure. "Darling, it's just that—"

Hasty words fell from my lips before he might make this worse. "Has Papa reached out to the senator?"

Blond brows lifting with ingrained snobbery, Ethan pressed. "*Senator Parker* would really like him to come."

No. He wouldn't. My father likes to play with his food.

Stupid, selfish, silly, happy Ethan whose antics offered me the sensation of *normal*... by the time my father was done with him, he wouldn't even know my name.

He wouldn't remember dancing with me in the moonlight, or laughing as we jumped on the bed like children. There would be no naughty smirks when his prick engorged at thoughts of what I'd willingly do to him.

I'd be nothing but a whiff of familiar perfume when I strolled by, gracing the arm of another prominent man.

Hand shaking, so subtle a betrayal of my feelings that no human eye would catch it, I set the crystal stopper back in the bottle.

And I felt... bereft.

Because I'd grown too attached, and I had known better.

Someday, this game of playing house would all end.

Blue eyes falling to my inlaid Louis the XV vanity, I hated that perfume bottle of revolting honesty glinting in the scorching afternoon sun.

How sad to be reduced to something so fleeting —crafted, expensive stink.

Knowing full well that Ethan could never grasp the fate he tempted, I let spite make pretty words ugly. "Next time I see Papa, I'll mention how much *the senator* is looking forward to the attention of his favorite benefactor."

Waving off my fake smile as if it were real and inconsequential, Ethan rolled his eyes. "When you put it like that, it sounds tasteless, Jade."

Because it was. The Parkers were extravagantly affluent in their own right, but it was nothing to the wealth the father of darkness wielded. And, after all, it was an election year... and campaigns were expensive.

Lifting up a tube of Chanel Shanghai Red lipstick, I ended the topic. "He's not coming tonight." Perhaps it was true, perhaps not. One thing

I knew was to never anticipate the moves of the devil. "But I promise I will mention it to Daddy tomorrow."

Another lie.

Tucking his phone in his pocket, Ethan bent down to press a kiss to my shoulder. "You sure you don't want to call him? It's going to be a fun party, you'll see. The president's coming."

And that was disgusting for a very different reason.

Not all of my former companions had been as sweet or as horribly selfish as Ethan.

He was a treat compared to men I was duty-bound to air kiss upon greeting. Aging men who had no memory of our long-ago, fumbling trysts, their tempers rattling my ear, or their slaps to my cheek.

One could write off such behavior as belonging to a different time with different rules, but I'd lived long enough to know better. Some men were just lesser than their gentler peers.

The current leader of this great nation, for example, had been just as disgusting, insecure, and chauvinistic in the 1980s as he was sitting on his fat ass in the oval office scarfing down Big Macs.

In less than an hour I'd float past him; I'd stomach the feel of his paunch pressing against my body as he leaned forward to smear his fleshy lips across my cheek. A shudder would run through him at a whiff of my perfume, and somewhere deep down, ugly, old feelings would stir.

Desire, covetousness... fear.

I looked so young, so fresh, how could shadow memories of my face flicker in the darker corners of his mind? The sensation of someone walking over his grave would be brushed off, ego stepping in to answer with an affable, "I knew your mother," or "I loved you in that film."

Though I'd graciously say *thank you*, I'm not an actress.

Not of the paid variety, anyhow.

And I don't have a mother.

But the human mind had to reconcile; it had to bend.

Weaker intellects made up the best stories.

So I would smile, I would laugh, I would make him feel important. And then I would drift away on the night air.

"It's past five o'clock. You know it's too late for me to call Papa, Ethan. He's very old. He's already in bed, and I can't imagine his night nurse would be willing to poke the viper. *He needs his rest.*" And the sun was still up. Even if my father were awake during daylight hours, he'd be feeding at the trough of captives stored in the Cathedral, not pulling on a tux to mingle with cattle. If I were to even mention such a thing, his laughter would rail down the phone line until my ears bled.

That is not an exaggeration.

Puppy dog eyes in a face that had graced GQ, Ethan begged. "For me?"

Smiling as if I'd fallen for his charm, my freshly-painted red lips replied, "I'm happy to write a check on his behalf. How much would the senator like?"

Before Ethan might do the unthinkable and mention a figure out loud, the pouting spectator who sat naked on the corner of my sex-mussed bed piped in. "I don't understand why I can't go."

Ethan's latest bleached blonde's timing was both perfect and awful.

Adjusting his bowtie, Ethan colored. I sighed—both of us having forgotten she was in the room.

And there was pity to be had for her. It was never pleasant to be excluded—knowing one was lesser than their peers, cut—that I understood intimately. But the three of us going through the paces knew why she couldn't attend Senator Parker's birthday party. Not that I, or Ethan, or even she would say so.

Low class mistresses were condoned only behind closed doors, more of a light joke than treated as living flesh and bone. They were not tolerated, or heaven forbid, acknowledged publicly. Even with MTV and feminism.

It was a mercy when we left her behind.

Where we might give her gifts and pleasure, others would eat her alive.

Speaking of food, my stomach rumbled.

But I refused to dine tonight; habit led me to wait, the need to feed ignored as long as my body might comply.

I still had two days.

Forty-nine hours to be exact.

So, now was the time for perfume, and parties, and stolen moments with old friends who had no true recollection who I'd been in their lives.

Now was the time to mock terrible presidents with artfully applied smiles, and know, *for a fact*, that they had the world's truly smallest, most pathetic penis.

Artfully applying a final sweep of black mascara, eyes currently a shade of blue, unlike my father's glowing red, stared back at me. Lids dusted gold, painted to entice.

From my bed, our blonde wrinkled her nose at our refusal to acknowledge her complaint.

Ignoring her huff, Ethan—exactly how his grandfather Gerard had done decades before—placed his hands on my shoulders, smiling over me while I completed my toilette. In the soft light of the vanity, it seemed a tender moment, the way his thumb caressed the side of my throat sweetly as he chided, "We're going to be late."

"You look very handsome in your tux."

How he fed on praise. That grin, those dimples, I could eat him alive.

Not literally. Humans were vile on the tongue.

And vampires shouldn't be able to walk in the sun.

Those two anomalies in my life were the very reason there were hidden cameras catching every angle of my perfectly applied smoky eye. They caught the facets of metal glinting off extremely expensive Agent Provocateur underthings. Why the gown draped over my massive bed, picked at by our resident pet, was flawless as she pouted and whined that she was not included... again.

Lips painted the perfect shade of red. Eyes blue as the Mediterranean Sea. Skin pale but carrying the undercurrent of a long-ago bronzed people. I was alluring enough to reel any hapless mortal to an early grave.

Yet I knew that no matter this soul-solid reality, beauty never mattered.

Standing so Ethan might help me into my couture dress, I meant the smile I threw his way. The slip of a satin-lined gown, the cold clasp of diamonds circling my throat.

He was perfection at preparing a woman for the slaughter.

And I... I was perfection at leading the room by the nose.

Knowing better than to kiss me once my lips were smeared with rouge, instead, my darling ran his fingers from my shoulder to my wrists, surprising me with a gift.

I loved presents.

The cuff was weighty, immaculate, and worth a small fortune.

His grandfather, before he'd died in World War I, had given me one just the same.

"I love you, Jade." Brushing a stray lock of hair behind my ear, ignoring our huffing blonde, he did something a man of his station never dared. He carefully kissed my red lips.

And was all the cuter for smearing my favorite color on his grin.

3

Sipping a third glass of champagne, my red lips quirked at whatever politician's wife Ethan was buttering up. The charm of a peacock, that one—all bright feathers and squawking.

Spell woven, he'd fully enraptured the woman to his cause with little more than dimples and a practiced swagger.

It was a ploy to aid the Parker family's political agenda. Trying to swing a senate vote in his uncle's favor would determine how far Ethan might take the night's seduction.

"Are you enjoying yourself, Miss King?" Watching the same choreographed dance across the city's chicest hotel's rooftop, Ethan's powerful uncle

—the mercenary and corruptible Senator Randal Parker himself—planted his bulk by my side.

I was not there to enjoy myself; I was there to overhear softly whispered conspiracy. Still, I offered a smile to the man of the hour. "Happy birthday, Senator. It's a lovely party."

View immaculate: the glittering evening skyline of the financial district's skyscrapers, the celebrity guest list, even the pot-bellied, bleating president holding court over the country's greediest misers, was pageantry serving a solitary purpose.

Clout.

It took more than designer garments, a pedigree, fine schools, or even contacts to rule this world. The key was in the small moments of ruthlessness.

Such as watching my lover seduce another woman and encouraging him with a sly wink.

"A pity your father couldn't join us." Pompous, fleshy cheeks reddened by bourbon and the night's chilled air, Senator Parker fisted his lapel.

I gave the unspoken complaint no weight, sipping from a coupe of champagne as I answered, "He sends his regrets."

"I was hoping we might discuss…"

Money. He was hoping he might discuss my father's money and how much Senator Parker might jam into his blood-drenched pockets.

"You should marry that boy."

Now he had my attention. Skating my glance from Ethan's antics to the scheming politician at my side, I quirked a brow.

Once upon a time the senator had been handsome and charismatic like his nephew. Now aged, and powerful enough to ignore the crutch of vigor, he'd entered his twilight years, morphing more and more into a jowly blobfish. It had been an interesting transformation to behold.

Ugly and terrible as he was, very few men could hold a stare like a cold-blooded Parker.

This offer of marriage... he wasn't flattering me. He was trying to buy my father with the gilded Parker's name. Which meant he knew something I didn't.

Mistakes, oversights, plain fucking up, led to unspeakable punishments I had no interest in enduring. Senators didn't throw their nephews at heiresses, no matter what the movies portrayed. "You anticipate my father will change factions."

"He mentioned—"

Slipping at the mention of my father for the second time that night, I demanded an answer from a man I'd been commanded to flatter. "What did he say?"

My eyes were blue, my dress was green, and my dark hair had been spun into classic elegance. I was everything memorable and forgettable all at once. I smelled of whale vomit and dead wood.

A born vampire who could walk in the sun—the weakest of my kind and also the most valuable.

Daywalker.

The only offspring of our king.

And I was afraid of my daddy.

For good reason.

When the senator went glassy-eyed under my influence, I demanded, "Tell me what he said to you."

"We have not spoken yet. But, immigration... he expects open borders. My platform... my base. I need to sell hate to secure the vote."

I didn't give a shit about politics, and my father didn't give a shit about people. Humans were a food source, nothing more. He demanded open borders because he wanted undocumented targets to harvest.

I did mention that he was the devil...

Angry, hating being caught off guard, I used the slight influence I possessed. Touching my hand to Parker's fluttering fingers, I planted a seed. "You're senate majority leader. Lying to your constituents is your only vocation. Promise them whatever they want, deliver what *he* wants. You don't want to disappoint Darius King, now do you?"

As I lacked the skill to fully enthrall, Senator Parker had already begun shaking off my pathetic mental influence. Ready to put a little miss in her place, he narrowed his eyes. "Well, you see, child. This is all above your pretty head."

I was older than him by decades. Hell, I'd fucked his grandfather! But that was neither here nor there. "Of course, sir. I apologize. It's just that I adore Ethan."

"Then marry him."

And that, a marriage, in this era of internet and images that even my people could not scrub out of existence, would grant me more time with my Ethan. I would not be easy to wash away. "I'll mention the idea to Daddy."

Sauntering away, the old man crowed, "You do that."

Thirty years prior, I might have let the thin glass of my champagne's coupe shatter in my hand. I might have hurt that man. But I already carried enough regrets and grasped that I'd have to pay for America's uglier desires once my father heard this... despite my obedience.

The devil knew how to extract his due no matter how hard I'd tried to obey.

Draining the glass in my grip, I set it on a passing waiter's tray, reaching for another.

Effervescence danced down my throat, everything gulped in a single swallow. Bubbly champagne spun in my belly, warmed me, but did nothing to slake the thirst I had ignored for the past week.

Having worked my pathetic resources on that flabby prick, working to squash the impending sense of doom, I was starving.

And no soul here could feed me.

Often, I'd flung away feeling of any sort that would not keep me breathing. Loneliness, depression, the need to run as far as I might from this horrible place. Engaging, handsome distractions had served. Obedience served.

Alcohol served.

I snatched another glass from another white-coated server, Cristal running down my throat.

Next, I'd marched toward the food. Caviar, candied bacon, delicacies too difficult to pronounce. I picked at the offered fare, smiling and making small talk with anyone and everyone nearby. Because that was my job.

That's what I was.

A showpiece existing only to overhear gossip and have my mind stripped at my father's leisure.

A fallible disappointment.

The devil would see me crucified for the slip I'd made that night. So why not exacerbate it?

Act a fool before the masses.

Pretend I loved it all, that I was friends with everyone. That I mattered.

Most of my act was for the single interloper who'd invaded my stage.

I saw him before he'd dared speak to me. Slurping down an oyster, assuring he had a clear view of how I sucked the shell as if human food were ambrosia, I sneered.

Of course, night had fallen. My kind had arrived.

Undying, gorgeous, and the last thing on earth I desired, he pushed through the crowd to approach. "Your father granted me rights tonight."

"Have we met?" I could never be sure, because I made no effort to engage with my food.

"I'll be careful of your fragile state." Beautiful chocolate eyes in a Nordic face. That man had been a warrior ages ago, bore the years and experience I lacked.

Pointing out my inferiority and documented physical weakness let me know exactly what type of male my father had sent to seed my womb. "How kind."

Leaning closer, the most beautiful male in attendance dared run his nose near my neck. "You smell of sunshine."

And he'd forgotten sunshine centuries ago. No born vampire would notice such a thing. "Let's get this over with."

"I have a fine room prepared." Smiling, thinking

he might seduce by flashing the tips of his fangs, he beckoned me inside.

"I know someplace better." Weaving my arm through his, daughter of the king of evil, I edged him toward the exit.

4

Arm in arm, I led my father's chosen stud through the city's finest five-star hotel, down halls meant for employees, around corners no patron should see. Escorting him out the side exit where the kitchens tossed their garbage.

A stinking alley infested with rats.

Stiffening, the male seemed to catch onto my game. But it was too late. I had already slighted him and shown the stranger exactly what my father meant when he offered me up for the night.

Dumpster to my right, some poor soul's vomit to my left, I hiked up my skirt and placed my forehead against aged brick. "I'm ready."

No panties. Dry as a desert.

Ass up like a cheap whore, I waited for the inevitable complaint.

"I earned this right! There is a room upstairs where you will serve me."

This old speech I'd heard thousands of times. "You were told you had the right to seed me. That you'd been honored with the opportunity to potentially father the next in my bloodline." And that was a fucking fact. "Not that I was to entertain your pleasure or orgasm. Get to it. I have laundry to do."

He wasn't the first to exact violence when I failed to live up to the fantasy.

Sexy daywalker reeking of bad perfume and the heat of sunshine. A poor vampire weakling who failed to thrive within the hive and bedded down with humans.

How lucky I was to be granted their old cocks.

It was the nose that always broke first. Smashed into my chosen wall as they hissed and tore down their flies.

Not once had my father ordered they be gentle with his weakling offspring. After all, I was immortal. It might take my body time to stitch itself back together, but very few things could actually kill me.

A violent lover certainly wouldn't.

And if he truly wanted the honor of fathering my child, no vampire male would take it too far. The womb must remain intact, after all. Otherwise, where would their little spawn implant?

But before my father's chosen might get underway, the air rippled with the chill of magic. Cursing at the interruption, the man dropped fang and hissed.

A portal opened in our *special* space.

Fuck.

At my back, my paramour stiffened, but wisely withheld acting out further once he beheld who walked through the gate.

"She's been summoned. Finish your business and go." Melodic, wondrous. I hated that voice with a passion.

The blunt head of a half-hard cock prodded my entrance. "I slaved for this honor!"

Blasé, cold, the perfect soldier... my despised guardian folded his arms over his chest. "Enter her, seed the womb, and make offerings to our God. Perhaps he will deem you worthy to try her again."

Under the Viking's breath the slander, "Bastard," paired with a forward thrust.

I didn't recognize entry, or pay any attention to the animal rutting. It's not as if this situation were unique. All vampire-kind were consistently ordered to fuck in an effort to keep the bloodlines strong. Even the pretty asshole trying to spend his cum in me must have been forced to mate hundreds of times, considering his age.

But I? Over and over, those who didn't know better assumed my pussy was some prize worth having. It wasn't.

A sleeve to slake lust within. A potential garden for the next life.

Not that I had ever conceived.

Every single day since I'd reached maturity, I had obeyed the order to try.

Miss a turn of the sun and be beaten. My father's creative concepts for torture were so extreme that I'd only refused to mate once.

More daywalkers were needed to be his perfect spies. Daywalkers he could flaunt when visiting aristocracy graced *the Cathedral*.

And his troublesome embarrassment of a daughter would become instantly disposable the next time I inevitably pissed him off.

I'd often wondered if I'd even be allowed the honor of holding my future child before I was murdered. Would I be granted the honor of choosing their name?

Jade was such a common stone, as unremarkable and easy to find as a pearl.

I'd hated that name long before I'd heard others laughing behind their hands at how little my father cared to choose something so commonplace.

At my back, the man picked up speed.

A grunt, a hiss, a grunt, and a rougher thrust shoved my slack body fully against the wall. Wafting stench of garbage, steam rising from cooling vomit, the scratch of vermin. He came.

No single apology for breaking my nose was offered when he pulled out and cursed.

"Darius will be notified that you received your honor, Calder." Chanting preceded the opening of another portal gate, our observer expending his magic to expedite the Viking's departure. "You've done us all an honor."

Without so much as a farewell, my horrendous lover obeyed.

Moments later, the air stilled, my paramour gone. But my handler remained.

Turning so my sex could be covered by falling silk, I pressed my shoulder blades to the brick and wiped blood from my healing nose. "*I'll be careful of your fragile state*, he'd said. Dick."

Edging closer, close enough that my stomach rumbled at his scent, the inevitable chastising began. "Jade, you wouldn't be so physically weak if you'd feed as you should. More importantly, starvation clouds your judgment. It makes you unreasonable."

"Malcom." I parroted his demeaning tone. "Despite my submission to having cameras all over my home, I do not enjoy having an audience while I'm being fucked." Angry, hating that this man had stood witness to another session of my degradation, I snapped. "You could have at least turned around!"

Faster than I by far, exponentially stronger, one moment Malcom was a comfortable distance away, the next his fingers carded through my fallen hair. "You need to feed."

How I hated that I jumped.

Against the undead, I was a piss-poor fighter. That didn't stop me from instantly shoving him so hard the wall he flew into cracked from the force.

"Don't touch me!"

He'd rebounded to his feet in a blur, completely unharmed by my outburst. Brushing dust from tailored black slacks, he had the audacity to smirk. "Pathetic, really. You can do better."

And then his fingers were playing with my hair again.

I couldn't effectively retaliate, because he was right. I was starving, and weakened, and so fucking tempted to tear into his flesh, that behind my lips, my fangs punched downward.

Embarrassing.

So I turned my head away instead, eyes locking on the dumpster as if failing to acknowledge him would make him disappear.

Lips at my ear, a willing throat far too close to my salivating mouth, Malcom murmured, "Give me your word that you'll feed tonight, and I'll leave you in peace."

Grinding my teeth, refusing to concede to such a blatant taunt, I hissed, "I'll eat."

Oh, I'd eat. I'd eat and I'd disgust the bane of my existence in a single swoop.

With the pitter patter of rats already creaking under the dumpster, as soon as one might skitter by, I'd snap it up and tear in.

Right there where he could see.

I'd suck that vermin dry and then grab another. Who cared that feeding from animals was forbidden, lowly? Agitated as I was, I didn't even care that I would most certainly be punished once my father found a hint of my action staining my memory.

He backed away at my agreement.

Once my eyes darted to where skittering was the loudest, Malcom knew what I was about. Silvery golden hair wafting about his shoulders like he was some goddamn phantom, he barked, "Jade, don't."

But I had already reached out. Fur filled my palm, and almost my mouth, before I realized that I held no rat.

A mewling kitten, dropped before I might scream.

Blood drained from my face. Vampire pale, I stared in horror as the feline scampered back to its hiding place, and I felt a thing I was forbidden from feeling.

"Look at me, Jade." Why did he dare sound so sympathetic? "The cat's gone. Look at me."

Gowned in Chanel couture, prettied, and coiffed,

with cum running down my thigh, I didn't even attempt to pretend that we both didn't know why I trembled.

"It's gone. It's okay."

Before his fingertips might ghost over my shoulder, before I might have embarrassed myself further, I snapped. "I told you not to touch me!"

Hand hovering, still as the corpse he was, Malcom obeyed. He even took two steps back. Only then did I make my eyes track from that sliver of dark under the dumpster to look at his face.

Like a carved marble statue, beautiful in the same unearthly way all undead were beautiful. It was like staring at God's favorite angel. Outranking almost every last withered soul in the hive, he'd never fallen into the habit of outlandish costumes.

Slacks, a fitted sweater. Utilitarian yet impeccably tailored.

And pity.

He was wearing pity on his impossibly attractive face. "It's ten minutes to midnight. I'll count this last mating towards your debt for tomorrow."

I would not let my wet eyes spill. "Fuck off, Malcom. If you think I'm falling for that, you're going to be disappointed."

His face returned to its normal state of smugness. "You're due home at sundown."

Wiping my nose on the back of my hand, I

sighed at the ruin this evening had made of my dress. "And you're reminding me of a standing appointment why?"

"It is my duty to inform you when you have been summoned."

The exact thing he'd announced when he'd intruded on the Viking's interlude. "I see."

He'd interrupted on purpose. Technically he had not broken any rules. I hated when he did that.

Eyes like starlight, jaw flexing, Malcom dared another modicum of emotion. "Do you recall the exact reason why you dislike me, because I can't?"

I had no intention of playing this game with him.

But he muttered on, running a hand through his hair. "I remember *that day*. Why you grew upset when you saw a cat. I remember that you were wearing a blue dress with a red bow."

If his reason for existence was to torment me, he was doing a phenomenal job. "Funny that you remember that dress but don't remember why you sicken me."

"Funny that we remember anything..." The anger on his face washed away into deep consideration. Crossing his arms over his chest, my custodian sighed. "You haven't even reached a century in age, Jade. You're still such a blind, inexperienced child. Acting out without thinking. Refusing to eat. Pouting."

The light in his eyes, it was as if he thought I were cute. There was no reason I had to stand there and bear it. Brushing past, I made to exit the alley.

"I'll throw you a portal, Jade."

The very thought of taking Malcom's magical charity made me want to scream. "I'll walk. Thanks."

Despite my rejection, he cast a gate at the mouth of the alley, leaving me no other option. "If you'd have eaten, you'd have been able to summon your own."

Fucking prick.

5

Disobedient and ego bruised, I broke my promise to Malcom. I didn't feed.

Not on rats, not on cats…

Not on vampires.

Stomach churning with acid, drenched by the spray of a boiling hot shower, I let the magic of indoor plumbing wash away what had happened in the alley.

Malcom most likely watched me via pinhole cameras, waiting for another sign of weakness he'd taunt me with later—his team monitoring Satan's daughter for one slip.

Guarding, he'd claim. Watching over a precious asset other vampire rulers desired to collect to serve in their courts. Or eat in an attempt to feel the sun one last time.

Fuck modern technology and the all-seeing eye. What need was there for it except to pry?

All I need do was stand in the presence of my father and the devil would see every last contemplation, mistake, exchange, disappointment that crossed my thoughts.

Darius could tear the mind apart looking for a memory so remote and useless he'd done it only for his own amusement.

I know this because he'd done it to me.

Water turned off, I stepped from the steam and caught my reflection in the mirror. Nose healed and perfectly straight, scrapes and bruises long gone, any set of outside eyes would see me as pristine now that the deluge had scrubbed away the blood on my face.

Inside I was uglier than the pile of vomit I'd just been fucked next to.

I couldn't wait for the sun to rise, to burn my skin and promise me in the sting that no other immortal might come near.

The only company I'd have to tolerate was Ethan's plaything. The blonde had been munching a bowl of chips on my $20,000 couch when I'd walked through the door. Without lifting her eyes from the TV, she'd announced, "Ethan said I could stay."

Well, she was going to be disappointed once she

realized he wasn't coming home tonight. My phone had already flashed with a message stating he had a rendezvous lined up. Just like me, he was getting fucked for his family.

Unlike me, he enjoyed it.

His blue-blooded prick was balls deep in a sixty-year-old pussy who liked flowered hats.

Ignoring the beautiful blonde, satisfied that she hadn't seen the state of my dirtied dress, I shuffled down my hall and locked my bedroom door behind me.

Head throbbing, I'd bunched up my discarded clothing and tossed them out of sight.

Out of mind.

Like the kitten.

Had I been wearing a blue dress that day?

It was so many years ago, and that horror had been the ugliest moment of my life. Small details I couldn't recall, but I did remember the sound my skull had made splitting against stone when my father had flung me across the room.

I remembered seeing chunks of my brain spilled out on the floor.

Everything had gone orange, and I could taste grape.

Six years old.

A baby when I'd cuddled my pretty white cat to death.

She'd had a pink bow around her neck. She'd been sweet. And I'd been so hungry. The next thing I knew, the ball of fur wasn't moving.

So I'd carried her from my glass conservatory where I was made to bear the pain of sunlight while I slept, and entered the hall where my daddy kept court. I'd interrupted to show him, so he could fix her.

Standing from his throne, he'd been furious.

It was the first time I'd recognized his anger directed at myself. Young as I was, I hadn't understood that there were esteemed guests greeting our king. On no level did I grasp his embarrassment when the king's daughter walked in with the animal she'd accidentally eaten.

Feline blood must have been all over my face, I probably licked my little pouted lips as I'd pulled on my daddy's hand and asked for help.

"Daddy, I broke my kitty."

When he'd ignored me, I'd settled for putting my fingers in his, hanging on to look over the reason I wasn't being addressed.

A man with shining, long brown hair and a high forehead. He looked like an old oil painting. Distinguished, old-world aristocratic, and dead-eyed.

Too young to grasp his station, I'd offered the stranger a smile.

Completely failing to notice that the retinue

behind him and the entire room were staring at me, I'd said, "Hi."

Belly longing for food, I pressed against my father's leg and clung. I probably had even tried to climb him.

"This is your daywalker?" That man, that golden-eyed stranger, smirked. "She's precious."

I'd shimmied my shoulders at the attention and swung harder on Daddy's arm.

The unsmiling guest measured me with unblinking attention. "Does she favor her mother?"

Large hand settling over my hair, Darius, my beloved father, stroked my head. "Vladislov..."

That one word was the only warning offered. That, and the squeak of pain I'd made when my father gripped my fingers too tight in his fist.

"Come now, old friend." Vladislov picked at his sleeve, outwardly serene. "The little one means no harm—"

And that's when I had done it. Staring at waved brunette hair far longer and prettier than mine, still hungry, I'd instinctively sunk my little fangs into my father's tempting wrist.

Airborne before I might flail at weightlessness, my skull met the wall. Shattering. Large parts of what made me *me* spilled all over the floor.

I don't recall if I'd cried before his overflowing court. After all, half my brain was gone. All I remember is orange. A world of orange and the need to move my body away from danger.

No undead dared assist me, though I could hear my human nursemaid screaming.

To this day, I don't know if she screamed for me, or because that was the last day of her life.

Smearing old stone, over many long minutes, I dragged my broken body out of the throne room with my only functioning limb. Across worn, icy stone, down the galleries to my sunroom where day after day I slept in a glass coffin and burned in the light. I have no clue how I managed to get my body up inside that bed, but that's where I went to die.

Like a wounded animal working on the last dregs of instinct.

And I should have died. A long way from full-grown, the damage was that severe.

But with my head pillowed on bloodstained ivory satin, liquid life itself slipped over my tongue.

Careful fingers put parts of my skull back together. Unable to scream, I wriggled as he'd popped my eye back into the socket. Clinging to the stranger's wrist with the scant energy I had left, an orange version of that foreign, brunette man leaned over my bed and stuffed handfuls of pocketed brain matter into my skull.

While I'd fed from him.

Over horrific hours, I'd mended, and I'd cried.

And from that night onward I was terrified of my father.

It was never spoken of, not once. The next interlude where my stupid, childish steps had crossed my father's path it was clear he'd been surprised I still lived.

He had not sent his ancient guest Vladislov to save me.

More importantly, my father had never seen in my mind just why I still drew breath. Everyone just assumed it had looked worse than it was.

Pleased that his naughty Jade wasn't shattered after all, King Darius demanded a kiss on the cheek.

I had run away screaming.

6

"Harder!" I could not shriek it loud enough, could not spread my legs wide enough to make that joining satisfy.

Thrusting with all his sleek-muscled strength, his blonde standing by as she watched, a sweating Ethan pounded my cunt.

"Fuck me harder, goddamnit!" For three more thrusts, the poor human did try, until he came at the unrelenting squeeze of my pussy.

We'd been at it for less than five minutes, after I'd gone down on my knees and worshiped his cock with my mouth.

Because I had a *need*.

The third party staring from the corner had not been invited to join, which was for the best. She could watch Ethan pound into my slit and have him later when desperation and duty called me away. Internal organs throbbing in their requisite for actual release, my body sucked in human cum from a spent cock, churning it up at the gate of my womb.

And I furiously rubbed my clit, chasing what had been lost with Ethan's premature ejaculation.

When I did come, it did nothing to chill the boil —thoughts of dumpsters and vomit and violence the only thing that carried me over the edge.

Unfulfilled despite Ethan's somewhat valiant attempt to hold back, I closed my eyes and tried to melt into the mattress. I tried to breathe through the disappointment.

With a slap of my hip and what was most likely a jaunty smile, he took his weight from my body and did his typical post-sex stroll to the bathroom. He always took it first...

"Do you want me to eat you out?"

Cracking a lid, I peered at the blonde.

Technically, I had been seeded. There wasn't any standing rule that someone couldn't slurp it all out. But I knew that was past the pale.

Not that I gave a fuck in that frustrating moment.

Spreading wider, I invited what's-her-name's attention and let a raspy tongue play where I needed so much more than anyone in my penthouse might provide.

It wasn't until she tried to fist me that I'd finally bent my spine and screamed release.

Immediately, I'd asked her to stop. Sitting up, I'd kissed her cunilingus swollen lips as if she'd done well, and went straight for the freshly-abandoned shower.

Ethan would finish her off, I'd caught them tangled in my sheets more than once upon exiting the bathroom. She'd squealed like a champion porn star, and he'd winked at me, surging with silly male pride.

I liked the show, the fakeness of it. Both were grade-A pretenders.

Both tasted sweet when their fluids hit my tongue.

But she was gone by the time I'd washed and dried my abundant dark hair.

Ethan remained, dressed in a beautiful gray suit for whatever function he was to attend that night.

Smiling, I sat at my vanity and began to style my hair.

"I adore you. You know that." An eager puppy, all big-eyed and cute.

He earned a huge smile, one that grew stunted at his next words.

"Kitty's pregnant." Expression warm in the reflection, adjusting his cufflink like he always did when he was nervous, Ethan softly pled, "Can we keep her?"

Brow arching and like the perfect idiot, my brain failed to put two and two together. "Can we keep her?"

Kissing the exposed nape of my neck, he smiled against my skin before stringing a glittering new necklace around my throat. "Yes. Imagine the three of us and a little baby. Won't that be fun?"

...he was talking about a person, not a pet. "Who's Kitty?"

Ethan's startled chuckle failed to hide unusual agitation under his mirth. "You're kidding, right?"

He couldn't be talking about the blonde. "I thought her name was Polly."

The last bit of his smile dried up. Straightening to loom over my reflection in the vanity's mirror, he frowned. "We haven't played with Polly in over a year, darling. Her name is Kitty."

The necklace, the ambush of compliments and sweetness... it began to sink in. If it wasn't so disappointing, it might have been amusing. "And she's pregnant..."

A locked jaw, sheepish answer. "Yes."

Knowing my extended direct gaze made him uncomfortable, I refused to let him look away. "And you want *us* to keep her."

"I do."

Now this was something... that didn't feel at all good.

Slipping an earring into my left lobe, I stood. Velvet robe gaping just enough to hint at nudity underneath, I moved with the grace my thoughts lacked. "You got your fucktoy pregnant, and what you're really asking is if *I* will keep her. As in, keep her here for you." Knowing what his answer would be, but making him voice it all the same, I purred, "Since you seem awfully enamored with the idea of your *Cat* filling up with cream, why not take her back to your penthouse and play daddy?"

"You know I can't—"

"No. I don't know that. All I know is that you want your girlfriend to house your pregnant fucktoy."

"Stop calling her that."

"I didn't even know her name." Which made this all the more humiliating considering my unseen audience. "Why you think I'd be invested in hiding your love child from Senator Parker, I cannot begin to understand."

Gritting his teeth, jaw working, Ethan set aside the charade. "She was a stripper, Jade. A nobody. I can't take that home! Imagine the scandal."

Reaching for my phone, going through the motions as if this conversation were a quick chat about the weather, I shrugged. And I felt *angry*.

I'd never been angry with Ethan.

"Look. You have plenty of rooms here and the green guestroom already has a bunch of her clothes in it. You're never home and you won't even notice she's here. We'll get a nanny to keep the baby quiet."

Pinching my brow together, I turned on him, as if such an idea were totally absurd. To say I wish I had not charged from my room like a disgruntled lover to find that my expectations were not reality was an accurate statement. I should have been embarrassed; instead I was totally baffled upon arrival to the *green guestroom*.

Just as Ethan had said, feminine shit was everywhere. The bed had been slept in. Even dirty clothes were on the floor. Most of the scattered couture was mine—borrowed without permission by an interloper.

I'd known she'd hung around. I'd known she'd eaten my food and fucked my lover when I was too busy to do it. But this... carnage. She'd been living here, and I hadn't deigned to notice.

Abashed, when he found the stricken look on my face, Ethan offered, "I'll have her clean this up. We can set the rules. Manage her allowance."

Why did that hurt so much?

Like the viper I was—a true daughter of the king of deceit—I let anger, hunger, and humiliation wash away reason. "You are extraordinarily out of line. My answer is *no*." I lifted a finger when it looked as if he thought to interrupt. "This relationship has been taken for granted far too long for you to expect my feelings about a stranger living in my house would be blasé. A stranger, it would seem, who already is living in my house... I don't mind sharing you; I like fucking other people. But they are just faces, and pussies, and cocks. We are not a ménage."

And there it was, a flash of shame in his desperation. "I *love* her, Jade."

He couldn't. He was supposed to love me.

"No, you don't." Softening the blow, I put a hand to his arm and gave a gentle squeeze. "You may like her a lot, but she's no different than any of the other blondes we've tangled with. They all look alike. They all laugh the same. Each of them fawn over you. That's what you love. The only reason Kitty, or Polly, or whatever her name is seems special, is that this one got pregnant. Most likely on purpose. Cut her loose. We'll find a new one. A better one."

It was as if someone had told the spoiled boy he couldn't have a new kitten for Christmas. All frowns and hurt feelings, he said, "Kitty and I have gotten to know each other. I mean it when I say I love her."

Lacking my father's skill at making people

dance on my stage, I tried my damnedest to take that lie straight out of his mind. "No. You don't."

If he'd loved her, he would have taken this Kitty home, and not tried to hide away his massive fuckup at his conveniently non-jealous girlfriend's penthouse.

Lifting the cellphone clutched near cracking in my grip, I dialed security before I might do something I would always regret. When the officer answered, my voice didn't waver in the slightest. "I'm going to need my locks changed and codes reprogramed within the hour. Ethan Parker is no longer cleared to enter. He'll need to be escorted off the premises immediately."

The line clicked, Ethan raising his voice to me for the first time ever. "Jade!"

"You need to leave now. I'll have your things sent over in the morning." I'd barely finished the sentence before there was a loud knock on the door. "Be happy with your Kitty. Congratulations on the baby."

Angry, flabbergasted he was not getting his way, he sneered. "Don't make me choose between you!"

He'd have to learn this lesson the hard way. Just like me, he had no choice in this.

He'd be made to marry me. There would be no more blondes. This Kitty, Ethan would keep her as a novelty for a little while, and then he'd start to chafe. He was right; he couldn't take a stripper on his arm to the Met. He couldn't take her to gallery openings, or to the fine restaurants his kind populated. She'd be out on the street with a baby he'd conveniently forget he'd fathered before the year was up. Then he'd be back at my side, loving and funny, and everything that kept my nightmares away.

Until then... I'd survive.

The door opened, a familiar security detail entering my house.

"Goodbye, Ethan." Padding barefoot over cold marble floors, I made my way through the beautiful penthouse my father made me live in, and left Ethan to Malcom's daylight team.

It took twice as many hours to apply my makeup, my cheeks embarrassingly wet.

7

Sundays, from sundown to sunup, belonged to the Cathedral. Ethan had always believed I'd attended evening Mass, that I escorted my infirm, eccentric father to take the Eucharist and drink the blood of Christ. The boy had found it equally hilarious and appalling that I kept to my family obligations in such a way.

I, the sexual deviant and sinner.

And never questioned why he wasn't invited.

The man would joke that he'd rather be beaten within an inch of his life than attend church—that even his senator uncle had never made such demands.

More than once I'd been beaten within an inch of my life. So faithfully, I arrived on time to my father's seat of power and left thoughts, regrets, agitations, and dissatisfaction at the door.

No savior carried the weight of my sins here.

There was no worship on site, not of God anyway. A great deal of sacrilege took place in its stead.

Ethan would not have survived five minutes under these ancient, hidden spires. Buried at the blackened heart of the city, an entire block wasn't what it appeared. Innocuous row houses, well-kept and quiet. Picket fences and garden pots. Cars parked on the street.

No human soul would be the wiser of just what haunted the shadows here... just what was tucked behind those houses.

I preferred to access the hidden Cathedral through a less conspicuous entrance than a magicked portal into the warded entrance hall. A cab down tree-lined streets, a regular key on a Tiffany's keychain, a modestly decorated façade of a foyer, and a contract bound, recently changed servant waiting with modernity's tablet in hand to greet those granted access through my favored private entrance.

Heels clicking over waxed wood floors, I stripped off my coat, handing it to an unfamiliar fresh-turned, without breaking stride.

Cathedral

Fumbling fox fur and hand-held device, a pretty brunette whom I suspected had been chosen for her particularly stunning eyes, made a noise of impatience at my rudeness.

I never came *home* to make friends with new and very expendable servants. And hungry, I was in no mood to try as I might have decades before. "Is there anyone set for execution? If so, send them to me."

"Excuse me?"

Blowing over her non-question, I tried to shake off the itchy feeling this place pressed upon me. Impatient, I snapped. "The conservatory. Send me something to eat."

Having made my way through the townhouse, I reached the end of what hid my father's fortress from a city of cattle. Hand to a spike-riddled door more ancient than this country, I pushed the weight no human might shift alone. Hinges groaned, and candlelight waited.

We did things the old way here.

Well, it might better serve to say we blended some human novelties with beeswax, scented lamp oil, slavery, and the distant sounds of screams.

Many of those echoing shouts were of ecstasy. Not all though.

In my father's expansive region, it wasn't

considered tasteless to fuck what you fed from. After all, how else was his flock to make new little vampires with pretty eyes and bad manners? It was best to woo them first. Those always made the best contract servants. Forced changes rarely ended well. More to the point, if you're signing away your life to practical slavery for three hundred years, it was best to at least get an orgasm out of it.

Besides, sexual procreation was difficult, and wars that ate up fresh meat were always fought between ancient rivals and their flocks.

This time of dusk, few lurked around the Cathedral halls, the ritual of preparation *to be seen* so deeply ingrained in many of those who ranked highest here, that it might as well have been the court of Versailles. Like the others of my station, I too had spent an inordinate amount of time dressing.

I had to be perfect.

My father expected it.

A princess was a reflection on her king, wasn't she?

Even an outraged one.

Immaculate, coiffed, makeup flawless, and a new a glittering reminder that I'd get my Ethan back clinging around my throat, I looked the part. More care was taken with the choice of sapphire blue cocktail dress than I might spend on the red carpet for the Met's outrageously ostentatious annual costume gala.

Hair gathered back from my forehead, sleek and long, it hung from a ponytail so my throat might be bare. A subtle *fuck you* to my father's people—vampires who went to outrageous lengths to keep their weak points concealed with jewelry, collars, ruffs, turtlenecks.

Yes, I was physically weaker than even the freshly-turned, pretty-eyed female who still stalked behind me asking questions I ignored. Yes, I feed from immortals who could snap me in half on a whim. But none would *ever* dare.

Not unless they wanted to spend an eternity as my father's newest plaything. After all, the devil could think up extraordinary acts of pain, make a symphony from tortured screams.

A dark-haired servant—another freshly-turned contract worker—walked past me as I moved through narrow stone halls. The delicious scent of a well-fed vampire wafted, drawing my eyes for a lingering look.

Mouth watering, I fought the urge to feel the silken slip of my fangs slide down. Gums tingling, I repressed the need. I left the unknown immortal alone.

One, who unlike my yammering shadow sniping about protocol, knew who I was.

No damned soul wanted to be fed upon by a daywalker. It was an embarrassment of sorts every last member of my father's herd avoided at all costs, though none were allowed to deny the king's offspring should I ask for a taste.

All designed to keep them hating me. To keep me from making a home with the only creatures in existence who wouldn't die with each passing year.

To keep me lonely and politically weak, while giving me more power than any creature haunting this hellhole.

The tight smile the male offered, the subtle nod of his head said just as much. *Please, I'm new and already fodder for the ancients who toy with us at will. Please, I might be too weak to survive the things I've heard Satan's daughter likes to do.*

"My lady."

Those two words, and still the young female tracking me kept yammering. "You can't be back here. I don't have you on the list!"

Instead of helping a fellow contract-bound fresh-changed, the male slipped away when I forced my head to turn away from the appetizing temptation his very presence presented.

My hands shook, but my feet continued forward on the well-worn stone. Conservatory before me, head aching from denying the feed, throat parched in a way water might never relieve, I put my hands to the unguarded double doors of a room made of glass.

A room made to harden the soft skin of a baby daywalker to sunlight.

Before I might find sanctuary in my private indoor garden, the freshly-changed vampire female grabbed my wrist. "I told you, you can't—"

To my left, shadow became flesh. And before the youngling might finish her complaint, her head became pulp against the wall. Smell of blood overwhelming, a shudder vibrated from my spine to bloodless fingertips.

There was no preventing the excruciating way my fangs descended, long and deadly, behind my tension thinned lips. Eyes to the door I'd only barely cracked open, I tried not to slur through my teeth as I deadpanned, "She didn't know who I was."

Malcom stood stoic, the embodiment of disapproval. "Nor did you tell her."

Which meant he blamed me for the death he'd doled out.

Abandoning the blood-splattered hall that left my stomach loudly growling. Refusing, even famished as I was, to feed upon the dead, I left stone floors for sumptuous Persian rugs, ivory inlay, and cobalt tile. Victorian architecture made up my beautiful cage, the scent of growing things, and a room that, come daybreak, would be drenched with stinging sunlight.

Home.

The little glass coffin my father had once demanded I sleep in still had its place, untouched by time, yet polished to a sparkling sheen by some unknown slave in my absence. Edwardian couches, ancient wardrobes, tables set for a feast that would never be laid. Branching glass side rooms for sleeping, bathing, reading—every need readied and staged for immortal and mortal alike.

There were even trickling fountains granting the air a pleasantness that the sheer beauty of the room could never accomplish. No amount of sunshine, tended roses, fruit trees, or satin might break up the taint of this place.

Fisting my fingers until knuckles cracked, I grew irritated that the dead servant in the halls had never placed my order. No breathing undead meal waited.

What was the point of having a smart device in these dead halls if the greeter for the Broad Street entrance didn't use it? What had she done with my fox fur coat? If her blood was on it, I'd never be able to wear it again without salivating constantly.

"Jade... your eyes are red."

Malcom's impatience at being left unacknowledged fed my impatience at his lurking. "You were not invited into my rooms."

"I have leave to enter any room you choose to grace with your presence." He dared run his fingertip down an errant drip of blood his little show in the hall had left on my bare arm.

"Not here you don't!" Already I had him by the throat, his shined shoes barely scraping the ground once his back hit the wall. "No soul has leave to enter my rooms without permission. I know that for fact."

What a vision I must have made: lips drawn back, fangs glinting, and eyes as red as the demon who'd sired me. Holding one of the most powerful males in my father's guard pinned by the throat.

And he could have broken my arm, broken my body, at any time in retaliation.

But hunger made me as stupid as Malcom had warned me it would.

I couldn't truly hurt this man if I wanted to, and I did. I wanted it badly.

I wanted to tear into flesh and sinew, gnaw his bones for marrow.

I wanted to feel his last heartbeat while I sucked in the stygian blood that made him immortal.

I wanted to feast.

Reaching out, fingers soft because predators of the night were designed to be tempting in all ways,

Malcom gave my earlobe a tweak. "You should have eaten. You promised me, Jade."

Hating how often he used my name, I meant to hiss, but found my head turning toward the subtle *thump, thump, thump* of the pretty arteries in a beautiful wrist drumming by my ear.

Marble white skin, blue capillaries. A lovely delta spreading from a single, juicy vein.

The groan left me before I might rein in the animal inside. Tongue flicking out, I forgot the man I held by the throat, the one suspended over the ground by my sheer strength, and tasted my lower lip instead.

Pleasure waited with just one bite.

Fulfillment.

And I began to ache, *I was so hungry*.

Right there, right before me was a balm to such pain. Right there was everything I'd ever wanted.

Teeth sunk in, raking deep so cool blood might flow so much faster into my mouth.

Pressing that wrist to my lips, I gorged, sucked hard... drained him.

Until a horrifying moment of clarity broke though the frenzy.

He must have noticed when sanity returned, for the bastard dared stroke my hair with his free hand... Or had been the whole time I'd acted the fool?

"Take what you need."

I dropped him. I backed away. I ran the back of my hand over my blood-red lips.

And I could not meet his eye for the shame.

That was nothing to the utter dread that surged into my breast a moment later.

"Daughter," a living nightmare whispered into the room behind me. "How good it is to see you."

8

It had been five months since my Father had last approached me in his Cathedral. Five months in which I'd grown complacent.

Five months since I felt raw fear the way I felt it when his dulcet voice drifted over my ears.

Scrubbing my mouth of all traces of blood, as if that might make any difference, I'd made sure to straighten my dress before turning to curtsy and cast my eyes to the floor. "Father."

Robed, he still dressed as if ruling the ancient Persian empire from which he'd hailed, vivid, gem-encrusted red scraped over the floor. He came nearer.

"My king. Senator Parker has proposed a marriage between your daughter and his nephew. He seeks to keep your favor as he abandons your policies. Jade argued with the boy this afternoon, sent him to his mistress." Just like that, the only report of note I had to deliver was stolen—Malcom taking the credit and leaving me to look petulant, weak, and most importantly, disobedient.

For I had not made note of the situation the previous evening, too busy scrubbing off the stink of garbage and cum. Then I had played at bed sport with the human who'd failed to seed my womb for years.

Unable to resist the scratch of filthy fingers picking though my thoughts, I wobbled on my feet, regained balance, and tried my best not to resist King Darius' mental probe.

"It's unbecoming, daughter." I heard it. I felt it. I knew my daddy's words in every last cell.

My attachment to Ethan: the feelings of comradery. He and I, both servants to great houses. Trying to paint myself as if it were us against an unjust world. My righteous anger that he'd claimed to love a replaceable blonde.

"How many times must we have this discussion? Did you learn nothing from your time with Gerard?" As if loving, as if he wasn't seeking to make me squirm for his own amusement, my father chided, "Did that old corpse leave his wife for you? Did he love you back?"

"No." Yes. Yes, he had. He'd loved me and he'd

been sent off to die in the war thanks to Malcom's interference.

And that was entirely the wrong thought to have in the presence of all-seeing evil.

The taste of King Darius' displeasure soured the stolen blood in my belly. It turned my bones to mush. Even so, I looked up, certain my eyes were pleading for mercy I'd never know. "I wish to marry Ethan."

I wished to run away with him and hide where no shadows could ever touch me.

"Hmmmm." A warm sound that chilled my marrow. More beautiful than any ancient contracted to walk the halls of my father's Cathedral, the king of my entire universe sighed. The unbearable weight of glowing red eyes left my body to settle on my guardian. "Tell me, Malcom. Has she been repeatedly disobedient?"

My father's favored guard did not hesitate. "She uses starvation as a means of rebellion, but in no other way has she dissatisfied." Feet planted as if an entire temple were braced on his shoulders, Malcom was the perfect servant. The perfect informant. "I suggest a mandatory feeding schedule and the installation of rotated offerings placed in her building to attend her requirements."

A trough of unwilling and embarrassed immortals for me to nip at when I had a hankering.

Already my cheeks heated from the mockery that would be made behind my back should my father agree.

I'd rather starve, eat once a week, and look strong in the only way I could, than be forced to snack nightly like my brethren did. This *rebellion*, as Malcom called it, was all I had to own my place here.

I hadn't seen him move, but next thing I knew, my father's thumb and forefinger pinched my chin. "You don't look enough like your mother to please me, girl. Keep that in mind when you let your thoughts run wild."

Because I looked just like him. Same high forehead, same lush mouth.

The only thing I had of her was the blue of my eyes... when they didn't go red.

"I apologize." For being born the way I was.

Next I knew, my hands were taken, arms spread so my father might peruse my clothing. "I like this color. Next thing you know, black will no longer be the staple at court."

Black had not been in vogue for years, but my father had not sat his throne or paid attention to such trivialities for longer than that.

My thoughts made him smirk.

Pressing a fatherly kiss to my cheek, I heard my sentence for whatever list of failings he'd compiled. "Malcom, you've done well. Tonight she's yours."

"Sir," Malcom said with perfect reverence.

"Well, go ahead. She's failed with everyone else. Enjoy your reward and give me a grandchild."

To protest in any other way than the hysterical quickening of my heart and shallow breaths was unthinkable. I hated Malcom more than I hated life itself, yet still I turned, bending over the nearest table to present.

With my father as witness, my short skirt was lifted, lace thong pulled down my buttocks to stretch across my spread thighs. And then the blunt end of an extremely hard cock met the dry lips of my sex.

Quickly working himself in, Malcom took my hips and began a slow, steady pace. All the while I stared at the wall, unblinking, even when my father's red robes slipped from my door.

The snap of the latch, two more thrusts, and Malcom ceased the rock of his hips. "Do you wish for me to stop?"

Nodding my head, I was already sobbing before he drew completely out. Slipping from the table to the floor, too overwrought to be ashamed of such a display, I curled in on myself and cried harder than I had in years.

I wept at the feet of a man I'd never forgive, and

let him pet my hair because I lacked the strength to show him just how much I desired his death.

Broken by something so commonplace as penetration, I was every bit the child Malcom endlessly accused me of being.

Crouching so that his weight rested on the balls of his feet, he set his lips to my ear, whispering things I could not hear over the sound of my sobbing. Not one utterance made sense, just catches of meaningless sound.

But somewhere, somewhere between my gasps and choking, a single string of coherent, unlikely words broke their way through the gibberish muddling my thoughts. "This does not change how much I love you, my darling Jade."

9

MALCOM

And yes, I loved her. I loved her with my entire being. For a century I'd watched her every breath and counted the beats of her heart. I'd broken her, I'd hurt her, and I'd done every evil thing possible to keep her alive.

Because my Jade was so young and so foolish. So goddamn blind.

If she only knew what I'd sacrificed, what I still gave, to keep her safe. What do I care if she hates me? Jade doesn't need to love me back. I love her enough for both of us.

"You will eat now."

"Get out, Malcom!" Crouched down at my feet, she tore at her hair as if to erase my touch, ruining the sleek ponytail she'd worn to mock those she secretly wished would accept her. And, again, I loved her enough to make up for every last immortal's loathing of their princess.

"Your father, *your king*, decreed that you are mine tonight. A specific period of time, Jade. The sun won't rise for many hours yet. You will eat. You will bathe. You will converse with me."

It was as if I had said something utterly inconceivable. Blue eyes ringed in red, bloodshot from crying, and unbearably beautiful, turned up. She looked at me. Right at me. And could not see what stood before her.

And I knew why. I knew what tricks Darius played. How many times he'd written and rewritten what memories this female possessed, how many times he'd altered her and coerced the ugliest parts of her psyche to come forth.

And even those parts were beautiful.

She was a creature of his twisted design, as selfish and proud and cruel as he could make her. But even he could only push so far. In the wreckage of his mental machinations, under all of it, Jade was still Jade.

My Jade.

Who for the first time in almost a century, I got to have for the night. *To have*, not to guard. Mine until sunrise. All because I understood the games and she did not.

"You may feed from me." I straightened, imperious and imposing as those wet eyes measured my stature. "Or I can summon another."

Without thinking, without understanding the true reason why she picked cruelty, why she chose exactly as I knew she would, Jade named, "The fresh-changed male from the hall. I want him."

What she wanted, deep down, was to irritate me. Because no matter what her father stripped from her memories, *she knew*. Somewhere in that mess, she knew she was mine, and desired a display of my regard.

Spying from the shadows, I'd seen the way she'd salivated for the male. And yes, I was envious—black blood boiling jealousy I'd never expose. Not where the Devil might see.

Here minds must be kept blank. Here one never lied.

After all, the truth could conceal far more than any subterfuge. Jade was too free with her feelings, those fleeting childlike things.

Even that I loved about her.

My blind little mistress still had her panties caught around her thighs, I could almost see a sliver of her beautiful cunt. I certainly could smell it.

"Don't look at me like that." Her whip-like snap, her embarrassment and anger... even after all her lovers, she was still so *innocent*.

"You're beautiful, Jade." Especially when she blushed.

Finding her outrage and pulling it about the sad, frightened, and cracked parts of herself, she filled weakness with rage. Glue settled into a damaged spirit, my princess lashing out. "I hate you."

"That can't be helped."

She hated when my voice remained even in the face of her anger. *Hated it*. But what was I supposed to do, quote sonnets to her? Sing? I was forbidden from courting her. I was forbidden from wooing her.

Darius knew.

He'd seen it when I'd first set eyes on the infant, and he'd laughed. A pealing, cackle of evil mirth I could still hear echo between my ears. The honor of guarding his offspring, the demotion from favored assassin, assured I'd know torment every waking hour. Forced to watch her fall in love, forced to see her fucked by multitudes. Forced to watch her father use her in the most horrendous of ways.

I had made mistakes over the last century, and she had paid for them. But I am also the only reason she still breathed.

My aching cock had been in her for two minutes, forty-seven seconds. I could have come on that first thrust... but it would have only made her sad.

My *starving* cock had been in her after a century of longing, and it had been done to punish us both.

I wouldn't fail her again, but I was also not giving up my night of her company. "Come now, Jade." Helping her stand, I dared much. Lace in my fingers, I pulled up her panties, my features perfectly controlled.

Hers… were not.

Batting my hands away, she pulled down her skirt and put as much distance between us as she could. Straight to a side table bearing a decanter of her favorite wine she went—difficult to acquire wine I had procured for her and ordered to be available in her rooms. It was difficult to acquire because I had bought every last bottle I could find the very night I'd first seen her try it. Three cellars in this city were packed with cases of the rare vintage, doled out by me for her without her knowledge.

Red fluid hit her tongue, that moment of recognition, the flicker of appreciation when the flavor profile worked its magic. It calmed her, just enough.

These little things. These small moments I gave her…

"Repair your appearance before Lawrence arrives. Should you let him live, you don't want there to be talk."

Exasperated, she kept her back to me yet snarled over her shoulder. "I'm not going to kill him."

That remained to be seen.

She fed like the demon who'd bred her. Not always, and the lad had a greater chance of survival considering she'd already had a taste of me. But when she starved, as she was wont to do, she was as messy as a freshly-turned babe.

Pride, alluring and adorable, Jade reeked of it as she smoothed her hair. Silver handled brush *I had obtained* from a long-dead Russian noble in her hand, ran through jet locks. All that raven glory was caught up again, tied back, beautiful, vulnerable throat on display. Almost every trinket in this room, every last treasure, an unknown gift from me.

A knock came to the door.

Jade poured herself another glass of wine. She made the nervous male wait.

Cruel.

Maybe she would let him live…

On that note, I was wrong. Detached from the scene, unmoving from the same spot where I'd penetrated her thirty-eight minutes fifty-four seconds ago, I stood by as she unleashed what she really was on the boy.

His first mistake was trying to fight back when she'd drained him just a little too much. It was the only time Jade was stronger than the rest of us, and whatever deeply set inferiority her father had fostered made a bully of the starved girl.

The harder they fought, the more violent she grew, the deeper she drank. Someone should have warned the child. Daywalkers couldn't help but kill.

When it was done, when her dress was ruined with immortal blood and the life had gone out of the rival male's eyes, the flash of regret in hers came. As it always did.

I would have killed him outside of these rooms, my jealousy in that moment was so acute. I longed to wrench his head from his shoulders, to tear off the cock she'd ridden as she'd feasted. She'd made him cum in his frenzy to survive her.

Sexual quota met for the night, but there wouldn't be a child.

Jade would carry no male's child but mine. We had eternity to assure it.

Disengaging from the corpse, its sorry, flaccid cock falling from her body, Jade failed to disguise her self-loathing.

My feet began to move, carrying me toward her because I could never resist. "Bathe yourself. I shall choose what you will wear."

Voice small, she stared down at what she'd done. "Please leave me alone, Malcom."

Never. Never for a single instant was she ever free of me. "No."

"You've made your point!" The nearest treasure

went flying, shattering against the conservatory's bullet proof glass.

A Fabergé egg. Irreplaceable. I'd acquired it for her tenth birthday.

Ignoring her common outburst, I refilled her abandoned glass of wine, wondering what it was about that vintage that pleased her so profoundly. I'd never had it on my tongue, not when it was for her.

Someday I'd taste Jade's after she'd consumed this drink. Maybe it would perfume her flavor. Maybe it would calm her when I drank from that perfect vein between her creamy thighs.

She took the offered glass, vibrant eyes weighing the temptation to throw it in my face. Instead she sipped, rinsing the taste of that lesser male from her mouth.

"Take a bath." Wash the stink of another off your skin. "You've had a *complicated* day. You'll feel better if you allow your body to relax."

I love you. I love you so much that I broke an almost century-long pact and whispered it in your ear while you wept.

"I'll clean this up." Already I was dragging the corpse by the ankle toward her door. Servants would be called and the blood removed. Ours was an efficient hell.

Frustrated, tired, my darling said, "Malcom. You don't have to stay…"

"Your father ordered me to give him a grandchild." And these rooms were made of glass, the moon was high, and very little was more interesting for my people to watch, to hate, and to gossip about. Should I leave, it would cause her more harm than good.

"But I..." Blue eyes darting toward the door I'd flung the corpse of her feast through, all the color drained from her face. "I already..."

She would not be getting away from this. I'd watched every breath of her life and knew every last trick she'd used to humiliate the others. Not a single one would work on me. "There are ways to assure you enjoy it."

I knew exactly where to touch her, what pressure she preferred, the order of strokes that would make her scream my name. There was not a single act of coitus she'd participated in that I had not viewed. With modern technology, I even had recordings of the best, so that I might study them and prepare.

Fresh tears, real tears began to gather in her gaze, and then she pled, she pled beautifully. "My father promised me he'd never let you have me."

What was there to say? Only the truth. I'd literally just penetrated her before him. "He is the king of lies."

And the things she'd done to earn that promise, the humans she'd allowed sully her skin. Another fragment of her pride crumbled, another flash of the real Jade shining through from underneath.

"I've ordered lamb for your dinner. It will be waiting when you've completed your bath." Her favorite, prepared by a brilliant chef I'd personally turned in 1936 for this express purpose, because daywalkers need more than the blood of their brethren. "You will eat. Afterward we shall play a game of Risk. Beat me, and I'll allow you to choose a film."

A sculpted brow arched, Jade's hands coming to her hips. "You want to play board games and watch a movie?"

Is that not what humans did? Yes. Yes, it was. Jade loved human things, human toys, human bodies. Modern human customs…

It was adorable, reminded me of my long-lost youth.

I drove the point home. "If you'd rather, there is a hunt planned throughout the premises for tonight's entertainment. The humans are to be set free from the pens, led to believe they might escape, and chased for sport. A great prize is being offered to the vampire who gathers the most ears."

Like me, she knew what the prize would be "A night with me…"

"There is no greater prize than you, Jade."

Shifting her weight, my love took a step toward

her bathing chamber. "I don't want to terrorize humans and cut off their ears."

Exactly my point. "Then we'll stay in and avoid unpleasantness."

As she soaked in a tub crafted of solid gold, as she washed off the other male and her disgusting perfume, I chose her clothing for the night. Modest silk pajamas and a blue robe to adorn her limbs.

Hair wet, face devoid of paint. Purely herself with the artifice scrubbed off, she took a seat, drank her wine, and faced me over the game board.

Of course, I let her win.

The film of her choosing was *Seven Samurai*, a movie so long it assured the sun would chase me away before the story concluded. Smirking, I allowed her this rebellion, horrifying her a moment later when I drew her feet to my lap and began to carefully paint her toenails a soft pink.

I didn't need to read her thoughts to know she grasped it was *this* or be fucked by a creature she hated even more than herself.

I'm not a doll, her eyes screamed. *You can't just dress me up and paint me!*

Blowing on her toes, I ignored the silent protest, too caught up in the fact that I was touching her, that the arch of her foot rested on my palm... that it might be centuries before I'd be permitted to do something so intimate again.

Before dangerous thoughts might follow on that wave of realization, I switched off feeling. I became blank. Then I met her eyes and stated, "The new feeding schedule will be enforced starting tomorrow —every evening, under my supervision, until you can learn to feed without killing your prey."

Lips curling, a hint of undescended fang catching the light, Jade threatened me like a kitten poking a tiger. "I thought you wanted me to feed from you."

"The option stands." Chest puffing out, arms flexing as if I'd already had her pinned, I smiled right back. Unlike my timid kitten, I let the full length of my fangs slip down. "But even at your worst, you don't stand a chance of overpowering me."

"We'll see."

So I offered my wrist, knowing she'd reject potent blood half the females in this flock would kill to taste.

Nose in the air, she turned her head. Predictable. Adorable. And mine for another two hours.

10

When the sun's approaching rays began to pinken the sky, I felt the burn itch and scratch anywhere flesh was exposed. Still I sat beside my Jade, her film nearing an end, and her easy snores divine.

She'd fallen asleep in my near presence, a thing that had not happened since she was a child.

What a human thing to do. After all, vampires didn't sleep; not in this way.

We became dead, we even rotted. Another reason immortal vanity was an endless cycle. Wake, bathe and deny the rotting truth with paint, and silk, and rare jewels.

Coffins were not entirely out of fashion, they kept the smell at bay. Until our eyes opened, until that heart began to beat again, whatever damage done in our rest immediately mended so long as we fed. Death reversed. Beautiful under the pus, tempting once the worms worked free... I don't miss the days of digging a hole underground when moved to slumber.

In those foundling years, sleep could last for months. But with age came freedom from the grave.

With the passage of time came extravagance.

A windowless room where I might lay naked so expensive clothing would not smell of decay. Solitary and hidden in the hive while death took what it felt it was owed. After waking, bathing was a chore and a luxury in this era. I recall going years at a time, stinking putrefaction stuck to my furs. Not that it would be noticed under the foul odors unwashed humans emitted.

Even when circumstance required I'd lived in the mud, I'd always had a penchant for cleanliness. Typically, when I'd dined, I'd devour a family person by person, leaving the most industrious to wash, stitch, weave, or prepare whatever I might require.

Often enough, that person was female.

Had they performed to my standards, I'd even turn them so their service might continue. Well, unless they refused to stop weeping over their dead husbands, brothers, fathers, children. A lesson all vampires learned young. Don't waste eternal life on those who might bear an endless grudge.

However, more often than not, the females were relieved to be free of their yokes. Half in love with the beautiful stranger who whispered in their ear that the world could serve their every desire.

Hundreds of women I gifted with the night. To this day, perhaps a dozen still walked the earth. For immortal beings, vampire's lives were miraculously short.

War. Feuds. Humans. Earth too hard to carve out a hole in which to sleep before the sun might strike.

Boredom...

Centuries passed. True cities began to spring up, to offer hunting grounds and a haven for immortal delights.

Vampires became myth—desirable, eternally young, untouched by the troubles of the human world.

Glorified, yet every last one of us in this age was beholden to a master.

Those who lived ages, lived in even a way I—after century upon century—could hardly grasp. King Darius was not the only ancient.

If rumor stood, neither was he the most cruel. All of them were rotted souls on the inside, whether their bodies be beautiful or hideous. But they were also necessary to the survival of us all.

We were not a gentle species, and with such long memories, we rarely forgot even the smallest of slights, eager to exact our petty revenges. Kings were required to control the flock. Queens were required to enforce laws. Those who could not be cold and cruel and do what needed to be done became dust.

Jade was a terrible vampire, a terrible human, but for a daywalker... she was everything.

Could be anything.

So pretty with her lips parted and her chest rising and falling in rest beside me on the couch. Dark hair, thick and smooth as satin. I preferred her unpainted, unpolished, just like this.

With pink toes.

Had I met her when I was still human. Had I pillaged her village. At first glance, I would have taken her for my own, hefted over my shoulder after spilling my seed in her womb. Claiming her for my tribe to see.

She'd have born me a dozen sons, half dark as her, half fair as their father.

My mother and sisters would have taught her our language and marked her with lashes until she loved me as she should. No matter what modern history books say, women didn't get traded for goats. They were stolen, branded, and claimed.

I would have fucked her day and night until her

belly swelled with my offspring. As my father did my mother, I would have tamed her until she accepted that she belonged in my hut. In these modern times, males drew their women with food, drink, entertainment, gifts.

It was exceedingly unnatural.

Had I found her ages past, she would have earned gifts from me as she nursed our young. Stolen trinkets from the Romans, fine furs from my kills. We could have grown old together. Whichever of us had survived the other having been burnt alive with their spouse's body so united souls might never be parted.

I'd burn with her now in this horrible rising sun if it would assure she'd be with me for eternity.

She and I in the fire, ready to face the Gods of the afterlife. Finding the children we'd lost to fevers waiting—and her brothers, slain by my sword, would smile to find her joined to such a powerful warrior. Even there I'd care for her.

It felt like eons since I'd seen my mourning mother burned with my father, since I'd heard the songs sung.

Jade would have been happy in my hut after I'd filled her with a child or two, after she'd surrendered. And what a glorious surrender. Those who fought the hardest made the best wives.

Modern humans had no idea what they'd lost with each *advancement*.

Had her King Darius not prevented my rightful claim, Jade would have done well to be locked in my vault for a few decades, where I could take care of her, and she could grow to know me in the old ways.

Hate could be broken with a hard cock and a practiced tongue, and my sleeping beauty was a glutton for physical pleasure I was only too happy to dole out.

Hidden underground, with no sun to set me to sleep, I could fuck her for years straight, feed her from my very veins as I pumped her full of seed. Instead, I watched her traipse around a window-filled penthouse. Instead, I rejected sleep so I could lurk in the darkest shadows of her life.

Instead, I bought up entire vintages of wine, created undead to serve her, left trinkets in her room she never noticed... and painted her pretty toes pink while she watched a movie.

Our night together ended.

With unearthly grace, I slipped my arms under her body, moving so slowly that not a hair was disturbed on her head. Lifted to my chest, I took her to bed, making sure she was covered by a blanket that would offer some respite from the rising sun.

Daylight's rays might not kill her, but they still gave her pain.

Jade should never know pain unless it was to make her better. Had she been mine in that long-ago time, I would have only beaten her to guide her to prosperity.

Now I tucked her into bed, the vulnerable daywalker none the wiser. And I waited with her until my skin began to blister and the stink of burning flesh tickled her nose.

Casting a magical gate, I retreated from the cursed sun, straight to the pens to feed. I ate ten men in the twenty-two minutes since I'd been forced to be parted from her.

And then I went to my private rooms, to my monitors, to guard her sleep. I'd rest another day, perhaps in a year or two. Old as I was, I no longer required much time in the coffin.

I'd refused sleep since I'd first set eyes on her.

The very woman who turned over, settling into the pillows, and slept as if the thousands of undead in the Cathedral didn't want to see her dead.

Watching her, I pulled down my fly.

11
JADE

I hated waking up in my father's Cathedral, baked and aching from so much direct sun. I swear, the conservatory was designed to amplify discomfort, the glass panes gathering daylight to dump on my head and burn me senseless. To make me stronger, my father claimed.

What it made me was irritable. Head pounding, I sat up to find a fresh glass of water had been left at my bedside. Parched, lips cracked, skin taking on a stinging pink burn, I drained the whole thing with no care for who had left it.

Or what poisons might be inside.

Instant relief, but only a temporary one. I could walk in the sun naked the whole day through and survive it, but to do so would leave me weak, horribly sunburned. Fortunately, I had fed well last night.

Which was the last thing I wanted to think about.

In the main room, breakfast waited under a silver dome. Fluffy omelet with ham and... a teacup of *blood*. Fresh, so fresh it must have only just been milked from a vein.

"What the fuck..."

Beside it sat a note, folded over and written on fine paper.

Finish your breakfast. All of it. Afterward, your weekly commitment to the Cathedral will be considered complete, and you may return to your apartment.

Malcom's feeding schedule. I wanted to roll my eyes, but it was impossible to remove them from the black liquid, warm and smelling of everything I'd ever wanted. Rim of the cup at my lips, I sipped before my mind might warn me of the trick. One taste, and both my hands pressed the china closer so I might gorge.

In a frenzy to swallow every last drop, I'd begun to moan, to use my fingers to scoop out any lingering smear. And then I split the porcelain in half so I might lick the inside completely clean.

My skin no longer burned, my throat was soothed, and my eyes cleared.

As did my thoughts when not a single scented molecule of a disturbingly familiar flavor remained.

Malcom.

The fresh vampire blood had come from him. Which meant he was watching this, most likely grinning. That he'd mock me mercilessly later.

Fingers fluttering, I dropped the split halves of the teacup, checking the corners of the room for laughing immortals. I was alone. Of course I was. The sun was up. None of them could touch me here. But it still felt as if he were in the room with me.

He *had been* inside me.

The room still held traces of his scent from all the hours he'd haunted my space last night. Eyes back to a note written in his vicious penmanship, I found the arrogant scrawl such an obvious taunt that my cheeks burned.

Had I not been groggy, uncomfortable in so much light, and eager for breakfast, I'd never have fallen for his trick… like a true idiot.

Feeding schedule.

Jesus, was I doomed to drink my food from a teacup? Was I to be denied the throats of my prey?

He wouldn't dare! Such a thing was unnatural; even as a daywalker, I cringed at the thought.

Finish your breakfast. All of it. I could hear his voice in my head, his snide tone sinister. I could even feel his goddamn smirk.

I didn't even want the human food, just as I had not wanted so much as a bite of the lamb from last night. I was *full* enough. And I hated when he treated me like a human. Especially here.

There was no higher insult in the Cathedral.

Golden fork to my dish, I shoveled in eggs yet tasted nothing. All I got for my trouble was a sour stomach, a sinking feeling, and growing resentment. But I cleaned that plate. I drank the juice. Swallowed each crumb, and then I fled the Cathedral to find sanctuary in my home.

I found no such thing upon arrival.

My apartment waited, devoid of life when the door snapped shut at my back. Ethan was gone, his blonde was gone.

Blaring sports didn't come from the den, the smell the astringent greasy lingering of takeout stink didn't add to the room's flavor.

The house was dead.

My heart beat three times, slowing, slowing… slowing… until I was dead too.

And then that godforsaken thing beat again.

No messages waited for me on my phone. No notes taped to the door.

Ethan had not even sent a text, because he was holed up with his blonde bunny. And I could see it. I could fucking see his warm palm circling her belly while he cooed nonsense to a fetus he'd abandon with the first dirty diaper.

This was loneliness. That horrible, worming feeling right there. The hole in my heart that ate me alive and turned my mouth to ashes.

Sniffing, I glanced around the elegant foyer, and found I didn't want to go deeper into what had once been my sanctuary. Not when I'd have to see with my own eyes how hollow it was.

But I didn't have a choice.

With Ethan or without Ethan by my side, I had *obligations* to fulfil. Charity events to attend. Important men and women to sup with and manipulate.

Yet hours passed while I stood like a corpse in my foyer, staring forward, unblinking. And in all that time, still no messages, not a single apology from my lover.

It wasn't until it began to grow dark that I moved, walking through the tomb-like house to find my bedsheets still rumpled, Ethan's clothes haphazardly thrown around our room.

He'd taken nothing with him.

Not that I'd really offered him the chance.

And even that had not earned me a spiteful text demanding I let him gather his things. Nothing. I'd earned nothing.

Fine. Let him sulk a day or two, but he would come back. His collection of fine watches was here, his heirloom cufflinks, *his future wife*. His uncle or his father would make him come to me. And then there would be no more blondes.

Unless they came with a dick.

Perhaps I should even ensconce a lover under the roof, so Ethan might understand just how fucking lenient I had been. A lover whom I'd allow to wear Ethan's clothing, wear his watches, and claim my affection while Ethan was out fucking old women for the glory of his family.

"He's not worth crying over, Jade. He's only a human."

"Goddamnit, Malcom!" The sun wasn't even full down, yet my babysitter dared stand in the room's darkest corner. A quick wipe of my cheek with the back of my hand removed embarrassing evidence before he might see more. "Why can't you leave me a moment's peace?"

As my back was to the man so I might repair any smeared mascara, I heard him take a step toward me. Instinctually, I countered, stepping more into the light. But the light was fading, even then I could see only the last sliver of sun sinking away from the skyline... and this male... this male braved the sun in reckless and dangerous ways.

"There are going to be changes, Jade. Alterations to the status quo." His voice was even nearer than it should have been, so close I knew his skin must be burning to a crisp. "It would be best if you chose not to resist, and instead put faith in my ability to know what's best."

A scoff, a tired, worn, and unhappy laugh.

"You were raised by a human nursemaid. After she was killed, you were left to your own devices, sent to human schools, and rarely mixing with your own kind.

He could not be more wrong. "I don't have a kind. I'm the only known living daywalker."

"You lack the basic fundamentals of being vampire. You fail to feed until you're weak physically and mentally. And when you do feed, you devour without restraint, and leave a mess. More importantly, you enjoy your infamy within the flock. You enjoy that they fear you since they have been forbidden to love you."

I didn't need this right now. Not while I was stung. Not while the sun continued to disappear and stretching shadows brought my tormentor closer. "You get such sick joy out of this, don't you?"

"It has been discussed, moving you permanently into the Cathedral while reassignment is organized."

The blood drained from my face, Malcom earning my full attention. "What? No!"

I was going to marry Ethan and secure that family to my father's bidding. If all went well, I'd have at least ten years enjoying the role of being his wife. Ten years with a partner who made me happy. For Christ's sake, I had spent fifteen with the last husband and he was awful in every imaginable way. Ten years was not asking much. And at the end of it, I'd bribe one of my father's flock to change him, to make him as much like me as they could. We could have eternity.

As if he could read my thoughts, pity crossed Malcom's angelic features. "Your father would never condone it."

"My father disappears for months at a time. I don't even think he knows what decade it is. One new fledgling would be nothing to him."

Cold, dismissive, my guardian said, "The answer is no."

Fists clenched, my heart racing and my color high, I marched straight for the blockade to my only happiness. Close enough to physically challenge him, I hissed, "That is not your decision to make, Malcom."

"It is forbidden from changing humans from a certain class."

"Bullshit! Marie was the queen of France before that ogre Gustavo snatched her away. I can fake Ethan's death."

"And spoiled Ethan would run right back to his family. Don't you think a man of his cut would want to rub immortality in their faces?"

"...Then I keep him from them for a few decades until all his living relatives are dead. This is not novel. Many fledglings have to be locked away until they're ready to accept their new role in life."

Fire lit behind an ethereal gaze. "I'm glad you agree on that score."

What had been shrill dropped to an animal growl. "You wouldn't dare..."

"Locked you up?" Dressed in his typical spy-on-Jade black slacks and sweater, Malcom crossed his arms over his broad chest and smirked. "I would have buried you so deep underground that no soul but I would have known you existed. Hunted for you, fed you, taught you our ways... *properly*. Eons might have passed before I felt like sharing."

Now he was goading me, and for once I was not falling for it. "You want to talk about infamy? You've changed hundreds of females and left them all to scatter and stumble through immortality. How many of your children still live? Ten?"

The fastidious man didn't know the exact number, and I could see in his expression that it irked him.

Trailing a finger between the flexed pectorals of an agitated male, I dug my nail in right over his heart. "And I wasn't changed, Malcom. I was *born*. You've never sired a pureblood, though not for lack of trying."

Miniscule, the movement was so subtle. A slight cock of his head. "Is that what you believe?"

It was impossible to read that expression, leaving me without the proper dagger to make my next stab at such an ego.

In typical Malcom fashion, he spun the argument out of my comfort zone. "I know you were born. I held you as an infant. The first time, you nipped my finger and drew blood. You had a taste for me from that day forward."

Shuddering, I pulled my claw from his chest, and moved myself far away. The room went ice cold, my skin bumping, more shivers following. And now it was full dark.

"I... I have to get ready for tonight."

Why did he have to pursue every time I retreated? Why couldn't this man just leave me alone? While I shrank into myself, while I tried to rub heat into my arms, the bastard toyed with my hair. Just like he always did when he really wanted to piss me off. "You're not attending the fundraiser this evening. The excuses have already been sent. I don't trust you not to approach Senator Parker."

Screw that. Defiance stole my chill. "I'm going to marry Ethan."

It was hardly a whisper. "We'll see."

"If you try to take him from me like you took Gerard, I'll kill you." Slapping the fingers away he thought might trace my jaw, I dropped fang and made sure he heard every word. "Do you hear me, Malcom? I'll see you dead no matter the consequences. And then I will hunt your children, and their children, and their children. I'll see your entire line demolished."

There was a look in his eyes, something utterly unsetting when he purred, "Then you better start feeding so you might gain the strength you'll need. Not a single challenger in seven hundred years has been able to take me down, child."

And we were back where we'd begun. A feeding schedule.

"Let's get this over with." That's when I noticed the cut of his sweater exposed his neck, and my panic returned. "Not from you!"

"Yes, from me. And then from another where you will practice restraint. There will be penalties if you kill your dinner."

This had to be a joke. A barb because of my embarrassing slip last night. "Last night was an accident…"

Rolling up his sleeves to expose strong forearms, Malcom ignored my complaint. "And starting tonight you'll learn how to prevent them. Starting tonight, you'll learn restraint."

12

MALCOM

She argued with me for an hour, just as I knew she would. Jade argued, she threw things, she went through the stages of denial, even begging so prettily it took a sheer force of will not to grow hard and frighten her.

I believe she sensed my arousal anyway, where tearful begs were abandoned in favor of her making a break for the door.

Never run from a predator.

My speed could not be beaten by one so young or weak, and the violence her act inspired caused me to be rougher with her than I'd intended. Which in hindsight, might not have been so bad a mistake. Jade's pride was legendary; crushing it was nothing but good for her.

It also solved the dilemma of how to inspire her

to bite. This hissing, scrappy monster salivated for a chance to harm the male who pinned her in place and held her by the hair. Snapping a quick bite into my own wrist, I assured she'd latch with proper placement, and rubbed my taste on her mouth.

The sound she made, the half-scream, half-moan, and I was fully hard. Cock weeping. Just how I wanted this first enforced experience to proceed, I pulled her back to my chest, sat us both upon the bed, and wrapped the snarling kitten in a tangle of my limbs.

With her distracted by the feed, with both her hands gripping my arm so she might gorge, I was free to begin.

It started with a featherlight kiss to her neck, over her jugular, so soft it was only a whisper. Every night I would do this until my touch was no longer associated with whatever horrid thing her father had planted in her mind. Until King Darius undid this work, my attention she'd slowly learn to abide. Another kiss, and another, trailing down her vulnerable throat. Innocent as it appeared, this very kind of affection did not exist between vampires. Not at the throat. Never at the throat.

Unless they were *extremely* intimate.

Cautious with her, finding she was far deeper into a feeding haze than I might hope for, I set her hair free, and let my other hand wander. I dared stroke the daughter of the king under the pretense of comfort, and then I took advantage of a cruel man's poor word choice.

"Give me a grandchild."

Sitting beside my love in her conservatory I had focused on those words. Trapped behind stone while Jade slept in the sun, I'd broken down and rebuilt my thoughts until the only concept that might be pieced from my brain was that of obedience.

I was doing the king's will in this.

My touch ghosted between her legs. Soft, creamy thigh, satin panties. I didn't dare intrude past that soft fabric, not yet, but so thin a barrier made it easy to still tease. I circled her clitoris, so delicately that the flood of wetness that instantly soaked the gusset of her panties astonished me.

The girl redoubled her efforts to gnaw my wrist in half, leaving me to smile against her neck. This was what I had been waiting an eternity for. And this was what I would take.

Skimming my lips to the shell of her ear, I murmured warmly, "Jade. You've had enough."

Just as I knew she would, she growled.

It took every ounce of my self-control not to tease her ear with a lick. "This is your final warning, Jade. Disengage."

Have I mentioned that she's greedy? My greedy, little terror dared draw a deeper pull of my blood.

The delicious ache of fang dropping inspired my cock to jump where it was nestled between her cheeks, the urge to tear at that soaked satin shielding her cunt and fuck her through the rest of her feed so overpowering I groaned in delighted anguish. But this was a lesson on restraint.

For both of us.

So I acted.

Driving razor sharp canines straight into her throat, I hit a vein with practiced precision, and made sure it was not a bite of pleasure. Jade squealed, knocked straight from her stupor into horror, when I took a taste of *my* female.

She screamed all the harder once my wrist was free to twist us both into the perfect posture for feeding. Like this I could use her as I wished. She could not break free, yet her blood freely filled my mouth and warmed a dead heart until it raced.

I swallowed a single, perfect gulp. I drank of my love straight from the source. Not stolen licks of spilled blood left behind from one of her punishments. Not the desperate gathering of her tears on my tongue when I moved so fast she hadn't fathomed what I'd done.

"Malcom?"

By the Gods, she was so afraid. And I wasn't sure if it was because her life was in the grip of my teeth, or if it was the way her legs had spread and her panties had soaked. I cupped her there, warmed her before I retracted my fangs from her bleeding throat and let out a guttural growl at her ear. "You were told to disengage."

Her only answer was a whimper.

Last night's feedings, this morning's cup of blood, and her most recent binge on my wrist had already strengthened her, the wounds on her neck closing while I took all the damn time I desired, licking them clean.

Poor, trembling thing wasn't accustomed to her food being so much stronger, not after her beautiful fangs had found their prize. Not when I stood over every feeding she'd ever had, threatening even elder vampires to remain still or I would see them ended when it was over.

Ancients tolerated her brazen feasts. Younglings died.

She sounded like the little girl she had not been in so many decades. "My father will see you punished for hurting me."

I could not help my smile, or the touch of conceit warming my voice. "A master's bite is a common reprimand in training. If you don't wish to feel its sting, learn."

She squirmed, as if only just noticing my hand over her sex. "This is—"

"Tell me now, before I escort you into the other

room. Have you had enough of my blood to keep your wits through a proper feeding?" Strengthening my grip on her just enough to give a hint of discomfort, I drove my point home. "If you lie, and if you kill our guest, your punishment will be worse than a gentle nip on the neck. So think on your answer, Jade. Do you need more of me before you attempt to feed?"

More fight went out of her. "What are you going to do to me?"

"Why? Are you expecting to fail?"

Yes. We both knew she had zero restraint or self-control. "If you fail, I'm going to make you stronger."

Jade hated when I spoke this way. *She hated it.* Already I could feel her tensing even further, and considering the punishments I've doled out over the years, I grasped why. But I am gentle compared to her father... and oh so careful.

The fact that she wasn't fighting harder to extricate herself from my grapple, the fact she hadn't fallen into a full-fledged panic, demonstrated that my less than idle threats were working. However, there is still a great deal of bite to her question. "Are you going to let me up?"

Smiling into her hair, I consider how much longer I might get away with holding her so close. King Darius placed very specific rules to prevent me from ever earning her love: I'm forbidden from courting her. He will always unravel any progress I've made circumventing that decree, leaving the girl with nothing left but hate for me as he walks away laughing. It's with a delicate touch that I seek to upend and take what I can between his *visits* with his child. Considering I broke a vow by confessing that I loved her, knowing what that will cost me should my transgression be uncovered, I'm willing to bend the rules a great deal this round.

But even I can't break them.

Not yet, at least

"Answer the question, Jade. Do you need more of my blood before you attempt to feed?"

"I... no."

And right there I knew I'd won. She would kill the vampire waiting to serve as supper, and I would gain another inch in this eternal battlefield.

13

JADE

"I won't do it."

"You will."

The way he murmured his easy retort, the way I could feel it against the flesh at my throat... I didn't need to see Malcom's eyes to know they glowed. If my father were Satan, this infuriating male was Lucifer. A fallen, devious angel. God's lost Morning Star.

Again, and with every fiber of denial I might muster, I spat my refusal. "I will not do it, Malcom."

"At what time did you think you were being given an option?" Pushing my hair behind my ear, tucking it back despite its crusted, unwashed state, he allowed his touch to trail over the delicate shell.

Practically naked, hardly a scrap of silk could

hide my shiver. No, all I had to hide behind was old, dried blood and dirt.

I wanted to cry.

I had cried, in front of this man.

Seven nights of punishment, each progressively worse, because I couldn't... I couldn't *not* kill my prey. And this one was already sobbing.

A pure-born vampire child, no older than twelve. A terrified, blood-fat babe dragged into the same pit I'd been thrown in when I'd made a genuine endeavor to kill my guardian four days past.

It was the first real violence I'd attempted in all the decades of my life, outside of the feed. Every last cell, each singular thought, had been focused to a point. I'd sprung, used every pathetic trick I knew, and he'd... toyed with me.

Laughed.

Mocked each swipe of my arm as he waltzed under the best assault I could muster. Faster than a human's eyes might catch, our bodies had danced. I'd even drawn his blood. One single slice across his cheek, and then I'd been forced to watch his tongue dart out to catch the black rivulet I'd earned.

Mesmerized by the movement, I'd ceased flailing. I'd stared. *Hungry*. So many meals I'd made of this male in the last waxing of the moon, that I *craved*. And when I hesitated, eyes stuck on that tongue, he acted. My cheek hit the wall. Old, musty brick and mortar leaving the taste of old dust and pain on my lips. My fangs ached, fully extended and throbbing.

My body, crushed, bent, manipulated, went slack from pain as if it were pleasure. I'd then done something unspeakable. I'd turned in his arms, eyes locked to his blood smeared lips, the thief tongue who'd stolen what was mine, and I'd put my mouth to his to get it back.

Devouring what he'd gathered, sucking his tongue, scraping it with my aching teeth. Licking at his mouth, even as his cheek healed. I'd bitten his lower lip, wrapping my legs around his waist. It wasn't a kiss. I was wet and he was erect, but it wasn't sex.

It was devastation.

Senseless, starved for more, I went straight to the nearest pulsating source. I'd raked my teeth over a black-hearted pulse. When my fangs punctured, I'd come. And... so had he. Because I'd jammed my hand down his slacks, and it was only his greater strength preventing it that kept his cock out of the hungry cunt that wept over his crown like a dribbling poison fountain.

I'd fought to put him inside me, as I did with most of my male food. Habit. Survival. The quota.

"Disengage."

My cunt was still milking nothingness in that ill-spent orgasm. Sucking upward as if his spattered, warm spend on my lower lips might be dragged inside. Within my fist, the shape of his member, I felt it all. Each pulsation. Each spurt I aimed. Malcom's seed drenched my labia, saturated my swollen clitoris... his blood running down my throat.

I ground down, fought, and lost, more focused on receiving, of being breached, that my locked jaw unhinged.

"Good girl."

And though he'd already come, though my climax had begun to abate, he punched forward to penetrate me in that moment—pushed his spend as deep as it might go, and held me there, spread against him, full of cock, startled, and silent.

He didn't fuck me. He didn't move. Instead he made me feel him, twitching inside me, flexing his meat so it might jump, so I'd have to meet his eyes, know what I'd done, and feel every last inch of him.

"Jade. It doesn't have to be all violence or games." His voice was velvet, those glowing eyes warm as molten gold. "When you're ready, I'll show you."

What the fuck was there to say to that? I'd tried to fuck my food, lost my senses and my temper as he batted around my feeble attempts to end him.

I hated this male, and *I* had done this.

"You don't need to be scared. I've always kept you safe, even from yourself. I always will." His cock jumped again, as if he'd willed it to spill a second burst of seed against my womb despite a lack of friction.

This was a level of intimacy even Ethan didn't press. No, he'd always spurt and then jumped up to shower. He certainly hadn't plugged my body, held me open, and tried to talk to me. Not unless it was sweet platitudes and praise for the glorious things I'd just done for his pleasure.

Out of my element was an understatement. I had just tried to kill this man. I wanted this man dead more than I wanted anything... except perhaps my father's love. The strangest sensation crept over my heart, one I'd never had and couldn't place.

An unnerving desire for my mommy.

Whom I'd never met and was long since dead.

"Whatever you're feeling, allow it. But do not speak it out loud. You must learn to be more cautious with the opinions you voice. *Thoughts* can be arranged, words spoken can't be retracted."

Under everything was the very thing he'd cautioned me not to acknowledge. Because saying it out loud, giving life to it, meant that Darius would pick it from my thoughts and toy with it. Still my lips moved. "My father is never going to love me."

"No, he won't."

Spread wide, back to old brick, spine scraped, and pussy still full, I forgot my body, the mess I had made, and was too buried in thoughts to care. "And for eternity, I'm going to be alone."

"Jade..." Malcom spoke my name with such weight, as if he actually cared and *knew* what it was I carried.

In that moment, what was there to do? I'd lost the battle, I'd shamed myself beyond repair. Even still I had his cock in my body—one he didn't thrust or use to give me pleasure. It was just there, forcing me to recognize the incursion... so I did the only thing that made any sense. I notched my head back, and smashed it into his so hard I felt the bones of my face break.

The pain was excruciating, beautiful, even as nothingness stole in.

And I woke in this pit. No doors, no windows, no way in or out. Just a round room of dust and darkness. My shredded clothing from the fight was gone, no pallet was on the floor for my comfort. Empty, naked, cold, utterly alone, I took my punishment without complaint.

Left with nothing but my thoughts, without the luxury to which I was accustomed, without human background noise and social media and farce. A well-fed daywalker with a mind full of ugliness that was chilling to be alone with. What I would have given for Ethan's stupid jokes or irresponsible smile: any distraction from the mental racket.

Before my father had flung me against the wall and spilled my brains on the Cathedral floor, I'd had a wet-nurse. A human who lived in a state of terror that I assumed was normal because it was all I had ever known. She did care for me, and not just out of a sense of duty... or slavery. Her lap was warm when she'd read me stories. Her voice, when she sang, was sweet. I remember the taste of her milk in my mouth. But I cannot remember her name. Maybe that segment of my brain matter was left back on the stones, and I wondered in those lonely hours what else hadn't been put back in my skull.

Had I loved ponies once? Was my favorite color purple?

Because of my father's wrath, there were pieces of me left to be trampled into the floor by careless feet all over the Cathedral. There were pieces of me missing.

"Are you hungry?" Malcom. I couldn't see him in the dark, I didn't know if he'd been there all along, or if he moved through the shadows and magicked himself outside of the pit.

"No." For once I wasn't responding to be difficult. I really wasn't hungry, in any way. Not after the amount of blood I'd been coerced to swallow since the feeding schedule had been inflexibly enforced.

Light blazed, a single small candle that was over-bright in such a dark place. Dressed in his impeccably tailored and pressed slacks, a fitted sweater highlighting the physique of a natural predator, his typical expression, Malcom held the flame and looked me over. "Stand up. Come to me and drink."

It felt like the same conversation we'd had for decades. His demands, my pointless, irritated responses of denial. "Fuck off, Malcom."

"You could have cast a gate and left this place at any time. Why are you still here?"

"This is where you put me, isn't it?" After I'd attacked then molested him. After he'd penetrated me to make a solid and twitching point that I really was the world's greatest fool.

Malcom minutely tilted his head. "Answer the question, Jade."

Irritated he was going to make me admit it aloud, I snarled, "For the same reason I take taxis everywhere. I don't know how to cast a gate!"

"I have watched you cast gates since you could walk. You used to laugh and lead me on a chase through the Cathedral that I found quite… frustrating." But the way he'd shared that memory sounded anything but frustrated.

"And then my brains splattered the floor, and I forgot how to do it."

"You cast a gate last month, after a feed so that you might leave the Cathedral and return to your apartment before Ethan left for his business trip to Paris."

Absurd. "I traveled by cab."

Another fractional tick to his head. "And here I thought you were smarter than to trust every memory in your head. Consider where you are, Jade. Consider why."

Bare ass to the dirt, back to the wall, I let my head loll back. Lazy in my perusal of him, admittedly forlorn and equally apathetic, I measured all I knew. Like how this man had been responsible for the death of Gerard ages ago, and how I swore I'd never forgive him.

As if my thoughts were bared, he nodded. Squatting down, as if to exist on my level, Malcom waited.

He who spoke first lost. Wasn't that the common saying?

The perpetual loser, I broke the silence on a sigh. "How much longer are you going to keep me in here?"

He set the candle atop the dirt, red wax dripping, and began to roll up the sleeve of his sweater so his wrist might glow on display. "Forever, perhaps… it seems it's doing the spoiled princess some good. A quiet time-out until you feel like trying."

"I'm not in the mood to play with you anymore, Malcom." And that was it. I was tired, disgusted, empty, and too full of blood to consider the wrist he held out.

Soft as a breeze, his fingers danced over my hair. "Were you playing when you tried to tear off my head?"

I could hardly remember the rage that had set me feral. "Yes, my favorite game."

"Were you playing when you tried to fuck me?"

Head in my hands, dirty hair covering my face, I couldn't even try to defend such an unspeakable thing. "I have a quota…"

"Ahhh, but one you have failed to meet for the last three days." But this disapproval he so thickly poured on me was not about required sex. It was about the rotting bits of torn apart immortals that decorated my circular cell and perfumed the air. I'd failed to restrain myself even a little, and it wasn't for lack of trying.

As if I might explain myself, I muttered, "You've only brought me females."

"But you could have cast a gate…"

There was no keeping the cracking weakness from my voice. "What is it you want from me?"

There was no answer, just a long incomprehensible look that was hard to read by the light of a single candle.

Hating pregnant pauses, having lived a life of filling them up with false laughter or banal jokes, I didn't know what to do. What would ease the monumental itch that vibrated in my veins when he looked at me in such a way?

Unfurling from his crouch, he stalked closer, wrist out so I might drink.

The now familiar taste of him so near, the smell, and my mouth began to water. "I'm not hungry, Malcom."

"Good." Bumping my lips with the cool flesh of his inner wrist, he added, "Then perhaps tonight you might show mercy."

My teeth sunk in, as if my mouth were separate from my psyche. And I looked up at him like a dirty, starving waif as I fed. The entire time he held my eyes. The entire time he praised me, petting my hair as if I were some puppy.

And then I heard the crying.

The child had been dumped in my oubliette. A clean little vampire girl in a blue dress. A replica of the one I'd worn that day. Red satin bow, hair in curls. All that was missing was a fluffy white kitten.

14

"It's simple enough. Don't kill her."

But the sobbing, begging, traumatized kid was so frail one bite—even from a weakling daywalker—would probably rip her neck in half.

Thick, black, male immortal blood coated my tongue, mixed with the dirt on my face after I'd spat out his wrist to pace. Bare feet crunched over rotting limbs, squishing old meat into fetid dirt. Bone parting from bloated flesh squelched. I kicked a skull, half the face flying one direction, the bone smashing into the wall just as mine had long ago burst like an over-ripe fruit before my people.

The child screamed, clawing at the walls as if she might get out.

I ignored her, tearing at my hair, looking every bit the monster that I was. Clumps of black came away in my fists, bare feet still slapping through the remains of my last meals. Like some demon from Grimm's fairy tales, I hunched and hissed, aware I was so ridiculous that even I had to scoff.

"Whenever you're ready, Jade."

Assurance, positive reinforcement? Why the hell did he use that tone as if instructing me on how to play the flute? Just lift the instrument to your mouth, purse your lips, and blow. It's that simple, silly rabbit.

Under my breath, scattered, I muttered, "I think I'd rather play the harp…"

"What?" Real confusion was in his abrupt reply.

I was going completely insane, that's what. "Malcom, I will drink from you every day, from any vein you want. I'll do it on my knees before you. Bow to you as if you were my king. Do not make me kill a child!"

He spread his arms as if to call me to him, and I flew like a bird to his fist. Soft cashmere hit my cheek, molding myself to the creature however I thought it would best please him if that's what it took to get that little girl to stop screaming. Lifted, cradled, maneuvered so my lips neared the juiciest of arteries in his neck, I sunk in the bite he silently ordered. And I drank until I thought I might be sick.

No hint of weakness came with loss of blood. Malcom didn't stagger. The arms around my body didn't twitch or sag. I swallowed far more of him than I ever had before, past the point of my discomfort, and then swallowed more.

A never-ending fountain of black, primeval blood.

Full vampires could eat dozens of humans a night, one after the next like popping grapes between their lips. Malcom, I suspected, fed a great deal, though I'd never once seen him do so before me.

"You've had enough, Jade."

Truer words, even with my lips to his neck, my fangs in his veins, each swallow had a backwash of equal size. A vomit of blood that waved from my belly to splash against his skin for me to fight to swallow again.

I was shaking from the effort to keep the sick down. Overfed, for days... and still I'd torn the bodies apart.

And I'd do it to that little girl too.

Cuddling me to him, petting my hair like his prize kitten, he hummed at my ear. "Take her throat. One sip. Just one. And that will be the end of it."

But I'd run to him, I'd let him hold me. I'd drunk more and more and more. Hadn't we agreed?

I couldn't think straight with her screaming. Another wave of blood purged from my belly, falling over my lips to dribble down my chin like a cheesy zombie horror flick. I must have looked like the worst kind of demon.

I certainly felt like it.

Maybe it wasn't so bad in my pit filled with splintered bones and rotting organs.

"Oh, and Jade..." My hair was gathered in a fist, toes set to the floor so I was made to look up at the menace I'd smeared in filth. "If you kill the child, Ethan will die in the most diabolical of ways. I'll toy with him. I'll make him suffer, maybe for years, until his mind is nothing but a waste of human mush. And then I'll make you eat him too."

Fucking asshole.

Threats and mind games and blue dresses and pain. Cock and fucking and quotas and eons of slavery.

Child's brains scattered on the floor, the half dead carcass dragging itself to its glass coffin to die.

No more nursemaids, or cuddles, or milk.

My virginity had been sold when I'd bled as humans do. The man had left money on the table, laughing when it was over, and I asked for him to keep me.

"Didn't think your kind existed anymore." Because his cum had been tainted a soft pink from the breaking of my hymen. And he'd checked before tossing cash to the nightstand the brothel's madam would collect after he'd done up his pants.

His name had been Gerard.

He'd died in the war despite his family's attempts to keep him from the draft. Malcom had assured it. Somewhere on a beach in Normandy.

And in my mouth was a little girl's neck, and on my tongue was the pure-born thing that gave her eternity. She tasted of heaven.

And it made me sick.

Still I swallowed.

I always swallowed, every last thing my father made me do.

Staggering, I dropped the doll in the blue dress, half-dead atop my pile of rot. Her heart beat on.

Mine raced, raced so fast I was sure it would burst. Blood came from my nose, and my eyes, and my ears. It came from my womb just as it had that first time.

"Jade?"

Was that fear in Malcom's voice?

Bits of someone's rib cage jabbed into my spine, the whole of my body seizing. Pupils blown, I stared into the dark, whispering, "I loved Gerard."

Lips to my ear, hard body pressing mine to stillness in the gore, Malcom whispered, "There never was a Gerard."

15

When I woke, he was there. When I slept, he was there. I ordered Chinese takeout, he was there, beside me and silent at the table as I saturated fried wontons in mustard sauce and stared into space.

Malcom no longer relied on the cameras to track my every move. Not even the sun kept him from the darker corners of my apartment. He thought to *converse* with me.

As if sitting in Ethan's chair, moving out Ethan's things and putting *his* things in their place made him a fixture in my world!

Refusing to look at him, trying my damndest for days to ignore him, I finally met the startling clarity of his eyes, and said, "I don't love you in return."

"I know you don't." Reaching for an eggroll,

Malcom made a show of joining my dinner. He even took a bite, chewed, and spit it out in a napkin so quickly it was almost unseen. "These are disgusting."

It had been two weeks. No texts from Ethan. His clothing, his collection of designer watches, all packed up and shipped out before I'd been released from the pit. He had not come to grovel, to say he'd like to keep me.

His uncle had not emailed with demands for wedding dates. And instead of mourning like I wanted to, I was saddled with a lurking houseguest who'd dared hang his trousers and sweaters in my closet.

The male used my ironing board.

Made me coffee in the morning and brought me fresh croissants.

And he touched me almost constantly unless sunlight kept him at bay.

Even now, under the table, his foot pressed against mine. And if I moved, he followed. My routine was so programed in his brain that he handed me cosmetics as I painted my face.

He'd stolen my perfume. My credit cards. Every last bit of jewelry Ethan had ever given me.

When I'd demanded my necklace back, Malcom had deeply frightened me. I was pinned and his fangs were in my throat so quickly, I wasn't even sure how we'd gone from the walk-in closet to my bedroom. He drank without permission while I fumbled beneath him and gasped for air. It wasn't until I was weak and limp that he pulled away, wiping red blood from his mouth.

A new necklace lay around my neck. One bearing a ruby the size of Manhattan. A weighty choker crafted in the old world by artisans and jewelers long dead. It was nothing like the sleek, modern pieces Ethan's assistant would choose for me. It was a treasure long kept, hoarded, and draped over my throat as if he'd waited millennia to put it there.

A quick flick of his nail and black blood dripped down his neck. Warmth splashed my lips, the salt of ever-living flesh followed. Drained, addicted, I drank. Far, far more than I should have.

It was the orgasm that snapped me out of the feed.

The bastard had *dared* to put his fingers inside me, my skirt bunched and my panties stretched by his fist. When our eyes met, mine full of accusation, his thumb brushed my clit, and I shuddered.

"This time I want to watch you." And he moved his hand again.

It wasn't just the shock of it all, it was the hunger. There had been no suitors arriving demanding their chance to seed the vampire king's daughter. There had been no human males seduced in seedy bars or dragged into dark corners before the clock struck midnight. There had been no playful touch from a selfish lover or his blonde toy waiting to lick my pussy when said lover was done.

Starved for touch... that's what I was as I lay under Malcom's weight and felt my hips rock of their own accord to the pressure of him strumming my clit, riding the fingers that hooked and beckoned my insides to run with lubricant.

I came so quickly, my eyes on his, that I didn't understand what was happening until a cry broke from parted, swollen lips. Lips he kissed when dumbstruck incredulity took the fight from me.

His stilled hand parked inside my pussy, a cunt that tremored and twitched despite my horror, refused to budge. Even when I muttered a sad, "My father..."

"Isn't here.

Was that anger in the unflappable Malcom's voice? Anger toward his king?

"I'll be punished." Horribly punished, Malcom's house arrest having forced me to break several of the rules I survived by.

Fingers squelching from my fluids, the male teased every last nerve below. "Let me make love to you. If there is a child, there will be no reprimand."

"Jesus." Was that my breathless voice, my head

tossed back as if I might close myself off to all of him if I just refused to look. "No." I was going to die of pleasure in a blood-drunk haze of agonizing and instant lust. "Malcom, stop."

And he did, rearing back to sit over where I was spread and ready. Licking his fingers of my juices as he studied all that lay before him. "What do you want in return for letting me have my way in this?"

Was he out of his mind? I couldn't even stop the laugh that jiggled my breasts and drew his eye to the neckline of my rumpled dress. "The centuries have set you mad."

There was no moving him, by strength or by power. A point proven when his finger came to trace the swell of my breast and no grip on his wrist might stop him. "I'd rather not force you, Jade. Name your price."

"Did you think playing house with me would warm me up?" Anger set my heart pounding, narrowed my eyes, and layered a hiss in my voice. "You make me sick."

No amount of spite seemed to affect the man. In fact, he began to rub himself over me as if he were a cat in heat, soaking the front of his trousers with the tell-tale lubrication that drenched my panties. A full body massage with just a few carefully maneuvered limbs.

His weight on me. The smell of a delicious,

available blood source that left my insides fluttering.

Tongue flicking my ear, pelvis grinding against where I'd begun to ache for more, Malcom whispered, "Jade?"

I would never be able to live with myself, the shame would kill me. "No."

Knowing how best to disassemble me, the constant demon in my life offered a greater temptation than I could resist. "Not even for Ethan?"

My nails dug into Malcom's back. Lashes flaring, I drew in a breath but found no ready reply.

"Did it not cross your mind to ask me to change him? You wanted to keep him forever, didn't you?"

And then my heart raced for another reason. "But you said…"

"Give yourself over; let me make love to you, and I will see your human turned. A member of my household, protected by my name. An eternal Ethan to do with as you will. I'll even see his centuries of service are cut in half."

"My father…" Why did all my statements always circle back to Satan?

"Will enjoy the irony more than you can imagine." Smirking, Malcom leaned back so I might see his face. "Do we have a deal?"

"Yes!" I didn't even need to think about prostituting myself for such a cause. I'd fuck the entire city to have my way in this.

Unhooking my claws from Malcom's back, I reached between our bodies so I might undo his fly, but my wrists were caught so quickly I yelped. Pinned over my head, I was trapped again. Next thing I knew, I was being kissed until I grew delirious. And I gave, I gave all of myself to that kiss because I wanted Ethan more than anything in the world. A tongue tasting of my blood, of my pussy juices, of cloves and honey and shadows richer than the rarest Bordeaux danced with mine. Nicked on my fangs, he dripped heaven onto my tongue to mingle with a droplet of blood his quick nip had drawn forth from my lower lip.

I came.

From a kiss alone, sensation washing all the way down to my fingertips as his groin rubbed, and rubbed, and rubbed between my legs.

A curse—I don't know what language it was—crossed Malcom's lips. His grip on my wrists grew almost too hard, but the pain had the opposite effect. It left me wanting more, force and pressure delivered in a way Ethan's human frame could never supply.

"I love you." The words were breathed into my mouth, the softest of confessions. Malcom's ruination.

He was so hard. Even with the fabric of his trousers and my panties between us, I could feel the pulsating outline of him. I could *smell* him—the tang of cum yet to be spilled. His sack was so full, swollen with what he'd usher between my legs so I might have my wish. Thinking of it in that way, of his cock, of his seed, had me making noises the man greedily swallowed.

Provoked, encouraging him with my arching body and digging heels, a space inside me shifted. I felt it like a physical thing, an opening door I was forbidden to look through. Desire unraveled, it possessed me with terror. Unsure how to equate the two, or why I suddenly began to tremble, to weep.

To beg. "I need you to hurt me."

"Never." Soft kisses trailed down my throat, my shoulder, the careful drag of fang leaving just enough sting to soothe.

Ethan. I thought of Ethan and why I needed to stop hyperventilating and control irrational fear. I'd been fucked by hundreds of men: violent men who took pleasure in my misery. Shy men with fumbling hands and sloppy mouths. Generous men who coaxed climaxes from my body. Terrible men I'd been attracted to. Vagrant men. Drunken men. Men of God. Women.

A virgin's fear had me pressing my thighs closed, had me stretching away from an expert mouth and the weight of oblivion.

Fully clothed, cashmere sweater, pressed, pussy-soaked trousers, even socks, this male was more threatening to me than all the others combined. And I'd once lost a limb when my father's champion was far too rough.

I was going to come again. From nothing. From just soft touches and rocking hips.

"Help me!" God help me. Save me. Deliver me. End this!

"I swear to you I will." How earnest this fallen angel sounded as he spun me into greater torment. Wet, hot, his mouth closed over my fabric-covered breast. Nipple aching, it was undulated, worked. Suckled.

Tears were in my hair, sobs wracking my ribs. "I'm dying."

This had to be how the sun felt to pure-bloods. A blistering, searing incursion that turned a body to dust. But I held form, even when couture split on the claws of a vicious warrior. My panties, ripped by the flick of his finger. My thighs gripped and spread until my knees hit my shoulders.

Malcom, ruthless Malcom, twisted his demon's tongue through my folds, penetrated where his fingers had planted their uninvited touch earlier. And I screamed, deformed, and scattered.

One moment I was having my pussy eaten by a starved man, the next I was in hell.

The Cathedral.

16

One moment the world was up, the next it was down, travel through an unanticipated magical portal leaving me to cough up a bubble of blood. One immediately swallowed down before a drop might pass my lips and mark the ground. I knew where I was by rote. The cracked, worn stones, the stink of agelessness, rotting flesh, and everlasting life.

Evil, unseen and gelatin, weighed down all things in the throne room. Even the air refused to stir despite the masses gathered to watch a rare occasion where my father sat the throne.

A sight even I had not seen in decades. Not when I avoided him at all costs.

Yet there I was on my knees, the straps of my slip dress having fallen down one arm, panties sodden and sticking to skin swollen from friction. And I had garnered attention. There was no need to glance up to confirm that those vampires nearest where I had appeared out of thin air stepped back from my panting, bent, and objectified frame.

It wasn't before the dais I'd landed. It was amidst the crowds. Hidden by the grandeur of court dress and the press of many bodies.

Terrified.

I was terrified, and almost screamed like the little girl I had been when a hand twisted into my hair. Pulling black tangles by the root, subjugating me before curious glances, the very bane of my existence put his lips to my ear and snarled, "Think of nothing but the hate you bear me."

And I did hate Malcom.

How could he drag me here, like this, after what he'd just done to me?

Only seconds ago his tongue had delved demon-deep into my cunt. The bastard had made me come. Arousal, a single bead of hideous, naked, and plain truth, dripped down my thigh for any behind me to view.

I hated.

I hated thoroughly.

To be seen this way. To have my head held in a bow by strength I'd never match. Left kneeling in a crowd where all others stood over me, where they laughed behind their hands at me. Where they hated me. That's what the Cathedral was. That was the revolting malevolence fostered here and worshiped by all my father collected in his flock.

Pressing against the stone with all my strength, shaking from the strain as hairs tore free from my scalp, I gave over.

Daughter of the Devil.

Unimportant. Completely forgotten once evil incarnate broke the chambers echoless silence. "Vladislov, welcome."

Straining to catch a glimpse between the knees of those separating me from my father's gaze, my full attention was caught up in that name. I even felt an echo of my brains busting against the far wall as if reliving *that day*.

Waved brown hair, long as a woman's. High forehead, pointed nose, an ugly sort of eternal beauty. An immortal potentially as old as my own sire stood before the throne and didn't so much as dip his chin in deference.

I knew his eyes, I'd dreamed about them puzzling me back together. I'd drank of that man when he'd come to where I'd gone to die all those years ago. I'd swallowed blood thicker than tar as he'd stuffed handfuls of brain matter back in my skull.

The guest more important than my little life

when I'd made the mistake of biting my father before him.

The reason I still lived.

Perhaps I hated him as much as I hated Malcom. He should have let me die.

Corner of thin lips twitching upward, it was as if my mind were as open to the immortal as my skull had been decades before. I think he laughed at me. Not that his face was turned my direction, or that I had been in any way acknowledged

My gaze was forced lower, Malcom still as marble, if marble might vibrate with a threatening decibel too low for even vampire hearing.

Denied another glance of my long-ago secret savior, driven to bend in ways that left joints screaming, I found my nails uneven, dirty, and chipped.

Which troubled me in the oddest way.

That I was not dressed for court—lacquered, scented, draped in jewels for this ancient to see. Because I knew he would. Despite the crowd, *he could see me.* Under all of it. Just how ugly I was. And maybe he'd give me that last fragment of myself that had been left to rot on the ground when I'd been a silly child who'd thought her daddy adored her.

His voice, like his features, was unattractive in an entrancing way. Making something lackluster pleasing. "My faction accepts these new terms with open arms, Darius. The alliance between our flocks grows stronger with each tithe gathering."

How long could he have been alive to have learned such a trick? To manipulate so many with so little effort.

"And just what have you brought me, old friend?" I didn't need to see the throne to know how my father's immensity sat upon it. There was no more chilling sight to behold.

"We are beyond the age of chests of gold and favored bloodlines. Dreadfully boring as they were. Yet, as you requested, one hundred of my healthiest stock shall be transferred to your pens, for breeding whatever blood vintage you prefer."

"And one hundred of my human cattle shall be placed in yours." My father was a greedy man for blood. My own eyes had seen him fell thirty in a single feeding. One hundred was a snack.

All of this was politics, even though I had no idea what took place, it was clear the back and forth were practiced, unimportant yet required.

Father didn't want Vladislov in his realm.

And that I had never heard of a tithe gathering though I had lived for many years.

Though by the way his fist refused me so much as an inch, Malcom had. Everyone in the chamber understood what this was.

"Where is that precious daughter of yours?" My flesh chilled, the fine hairs on the back of my neck rising. "I have a stud who wishes to woo her. Of course, any offspring would belong to my house should he succeed."

"Which daughter?"

No hesitation came with the answer. "The sweet one."

Slander nailed those words to my back. Physically bowing, I felt the drill of *sweet* and knew the joke they made of me. There were no other daughters.

None living, at least. Had King Darius fathered others, they were long from this world. Or had escaped him through the ages, no longer counted and free.

Which was impossible when every immortal mind was open to him like a book.

Once, long ago, I'd tried to run.

Malcom had found me in minutes. Literally minutes. He'd brought me to the throne bloodied to dump at my father's feet.

He'd beaten me so badly that my father had not so much as lifted a finger to crack another bone. Knowing him now, I imagine Malcom thought he'd done me a mercy. My father could *do things* even to an immortal that could not be undone.

"Where is the little girl?" How strange it was to

hear a hint of teasing in Vladislov's voice. One did not mince words with the devil and survive it. One did not poke the bear.

A coarse, bored, devious, and light reply. "I will allow your stud to attempt to breed her, but there will be no talk of my daywalker."

"But I like her." Again, I knew the foreigner was aware of my presence, and had the sinking sense that through some strange turn, my father was not. "Why be so greedy? She was a taste of heaven when she sat on your knee. I'd offer you a legion, an army, any member of my court in exchange for the precious child."

"Denied."

The guest grew openly agitated. "Ten years."

I moved, fought to look up. Malcom twisted my hair tighter, clawing my scalp until skin punctured, simultaneously grinding my knees harder into the stone.

"Think on it, old friend." Though I couldn't see him, I imagined Vladislov smoothing his embroidered sleeve, careless that the man on the throne could see his head rent from his shoulders with little effort. "No need to make a rash decision. I can offer your kingdom much. And what is one, unwanted, burdensome half-breed? It would do her some good to go to the old country and learn of her heritage. I have a particularly vicious warlord in mind for her to tend. Instability on the continent affects even your Americas. And, of course, I'd watch over her as if she were my own daughter..."

"You'd find her lacking, weak, and insubordinate. Ungracious in bed. The complaints I've heard..." Was this really how my father spoke of me to strangers? To ancients? My mouth went sour with the shame of it, thighs quivering to close despite my painful posture.

"Sad news for my stud, I suppose."

"I have no interest in your stud's complaints." And the meeting was over. A shuffle of silks, the king of all undead this side of the ocean rising to leave as if bored of all he saw, all he'd lived. As if he had somewhere to go.

And go he did. The force of his presence lifting from the room. Those within sucking in a breath as if they had been denied air for an eternity. I found it funny, the immortal, *breathing* in relief.

The crowd began to jostle and migrate, careless feet stepping upon splayed fingers. Caught up in the tide, Malcom kept me still, like a dog on a leash by the hair. Tethered to be stepped on.

Until the room was vacant, as if all inside acted on some unseen order to wander away.

My father's throne empty, until it wasn't. Until the brunette foreigner in his surcoat and cravat, his thin fingers heavy with rings placed himself upon it.

And my heart stopped beating. Arteries stopped pumping. Ghostly white, I felt dread to see something so horrific.

"Child." He smiled at me. One perfected with age and practice. "Is it true you are disobedient?"

Eyes darting around, looking for the trick, the lingering vampire who would have me existing in a room where another dared sit my father's throne. "How is it that you have done this?"

Proud, arrogant, ugly-beautiful, in completely different ways from my sire. Vladislov offered a shrug. My father would never shrug. "We all have our tricks. What's yours?"

I don't know why this banter drew my anger, but it did. There were enough problems piled on my plate, and pieces of my brains had once been in that man's pockets. "I can walk in the sun."

Without taking his eyes from my face, Vladislov flicked his wrist. A kingly, courtly gesture, both demeaning and silly. "Get out, Malcom. You're not required at present."

And my hair was set free. Just like that.

And just like that, I reached back for my guardian because I knew to remain in that room would see me ended. I even turned, eyes wide as I pled, "We had a deal."

"But you see." Stretching his legs out from my

father's throne, Vladislov murmured, "He and I had one first."

There was no soldier more loyal to King Darius than Malcom. Not a one. Which made this foreigner a liar.

As Malcom backed away, Vladislov mused, "She is young, isn't she? An unopened bloom."

The one fixture in my life—the lingering, annoying presence of my custodian—walked away without answering.

The question had, after all, been rhetorical.

And I was still on my knees, reddened by the stone. I was dirty, disheveled, unable to look away from the figure in the chair.

"Stand up and let me take a look at you, little one."

Like a child, dusting my hands on my dusty dress, a look of shame about me, I did.

17

There was a hand on my face, turning it to and fro, but no one touched me. A compulsion to move that felt so real I gasped, even as I obeyed.

"I know what you're thinking." He murmured from my father's throne. "I could make you rip out your heart and eat it."

Those weren't my thoughts exactly, but near enough that I shivered.

Vladislov's voice became more beautiful. "You cried that night, the innocent tears of a hurting babe. I found it moved me. Old as I am, very little does."

"I'm not supposed to be here." In this room for this meeting. My father wouldn't want me near the Cathedral or this man. The power of that latent thought was so insidious, so all-consuming that my eyelid twitched.

A frown, the expression insincere when his eyes shone so bright. "Then why did you open a portal and come to me?"

"I don't... know." I couldn't cast portals! I didn't know how I'd come to be here or why Malcom had vibrated with *apprehension*. Why he'd told me to think of hate, and how easy it had been to fall into the habit.

My father had not noticed me. Because my thoughts were ugly and unremarkable in the sea of ugly unremarkable minds.

Hypnotic, a voice I could love moved through my spirit, my flesh, and made all the little aches go away. "Tell me of your father. Spill every secret you know."

And I laughed, loudly. "I know none."

"Ahhhh, child." The caress of that endearment, of Vladislov's complete attention, warmed me despite the chill of the room. "Start at the beginning, and let's peel back some of these layers, shall we?"

My story began with my head cracking against the wall, the sensation of my brain matter spilling out. The smells of the floor and taste of grape as I'd dragged my carcass to my casket. How a stranger had come with handfuls of me to put back in the crater. One who sewed me up with tar-black blood and careful attention. Freely, I told that man these things.

I spoke of beatings and sex. I unfurled every bit of personal shame, all the words spilling from my mouth like a corruption. Decades of my life purged, belched, made the air grotesque, but not once did Vladislov lose interest. He *listened* without speaking.

Uninterrupted hours.

Until I felt unburdened, changed.

Chin resting in his palm, soaking me in attentiveness, the man sitting the throne said, "And you thought you knew no secrets. What a vault he's made of you. Can you even recall half of what you told me?"

I felt so young then, nothing but a little girl in a blue dress. "I'm tired. I want to go home."

"Child, tell me one more secret, and I'll send you on your way." I'd tell him anything. Anything he'd ever wish to know. "What would you do to this Cathedral had you the power to act as you pleased?"

No hesitation, I wasn't even afraid to say something so hideous. "Burn it to the ground."

"With or without your father's flock inside?"

That was the question that stumped me, because I had no answer.

Hands to the armrests, Vladislov stood, moving like a cool breeze. Whispering past me he said, "Think on it. I'm interested in knowing you better."

And then he was gone.

Alone, barefoot and underdressed. I stood like an urchin before a vacant throne, unsure what to do with myself or where to go.

I never even heard his steps before a coat was wrapped around shivering shoulders. "Of all the places you could have traveled through portal to…" Malcom pulled me to him, wrapped me in strength and a niggling, itchy comfort. "Time to return home."

Portals could not be cast within the warded Cathedral. Antechambers existed that allowed the magic to work, but I had somehow, without chanting and without meaning to, landed in the middle of an audience.

I had done that. Not Malcom.

It was to myself I muttered, "I don't know how I did it."

But I thought of home and how badly I needed to be anywhere but where I currently stood. And then I was. My kitchen was a mess of takeout containers and empty ice cream bins. It smelled like human laziness and petulance. It smelled of several days gone.

And Malcom was there, having followed me through whatever magic I had unknowingly used, ushering us toward my room. Toward a bath.

It was dark outside, leaving me no sunlight to soak in or the ability to wriggle out of Malcom's never-ending touch.

Tub full and steaming, bubbles added in, it waited for me. And I stood there like a simpleton while Malcom removed my dirtied dress, my panties, another layer of me. I stood there staring forward, trying to navigate a mind that made no sense.

"I told him things." Horrible things that I should not have known, that even now flickered in and out of my memory as if imaginings.

"Of course you did." No censure was in Malcom's response, nothing but doting attention as he helped me step into the bath.

Knees to my chin I stared forward while he ran a length of expensive Egyptian cotton across my shoulder blades. Tracing the length of my spine, the shape of my ribs, dips and curves, taking his time.

He washed my hair, an intimacy even Ethan never participated in. Dipped me back to rinse it. Carefully combed through conditioner. Cleaned my nails of chipped polish, shaped them. While I soaked in heat as if I'd been frozen inside and needed to thaw.

I was incapable of considering Malcom's attention as anything unclean. It was impossible when my mind was spinning—full of the face of an ancient who'd opened me up like an unripe bloom. Too early, petals not yet fully formed, but free nonetheless. A forced bloom that looked the most striking in a vase and failed the soonest.

It took unimaginable effort to shift my eyes to catch the devoted gaze of my guardian. It was even harder to ask. "What deal did you make with him?"

Cupping my cheek, gentle, Malcom said, "In exchange for fealty, I begged him to save the thing I loved most."

A little girl in a blue dress whose mind had been tampered with by her father and was in such a riotous mess that I wasn't sure I'd be able to climb back out of it. "You committed treason."

"I couldn't let you die, cast off like... not when I've always known how precious you are." His grip on my jaw grew firm, as did Malcom's fiery expression. Even his fangs elongated to a startling degree. "I stood there the whole time he pieced you back together. Paid an eternal debt in exchange so that one day I could keep you. The little girl in the blue dress all grown up and mine."

And that sank deeper than any bite. "I've been everyone else's but yours."

I'd never seen this side of him, passion enraged,

so beyond collected I hardly recognized him. "You've always been mine. From the moment I held you bloody and fresh from the womb. He hadn't even swaddled you, just dumped you cold and naked, cord still attached, in my hands. I quitted your cries. Found you milk; nursed you blood from my fingertips. I hid you from the court except when your father wanted to prance his prize pony about. I've murdered almost every human you slept with, hundreds. I didn't even drink them. I just left them to rot."

This fairytale sounded so untrue I began to wake from my stupor. "My father would have never allowed any of this."

Not out of love for me, but out of control. He dictated every breath I took.

"Your father is an absentee king so obsessed with his treasures he forgets you exist for months at a time. And when the bastard is coherent enough to serve his duty, he orders you whored out—as if you were not the offspring of an ancient bloodline and precious. He had you lay with *humans*." The last word was said with such disgust, I felt it like a living thing in the room.

Malcom was not finished. "Do you not think he would do the same to our children? That he would not toy with them in his sick-minded fascinations with suffering. Darius has lived too long!"

This was some trick, some new game my father played. Sloshing back, water waving in the monstrous tub, I put space between myself and this stranger who spoke of *our children* as if it were some given. And I looked at him. I really looked at Malcom and found a stranger in his skin.

As if he might read my thoughts, he swore, "You don't need to be afraid of me."

At that I laughed, choking on bile, and I backed into the farthest corner my tub might allow. "You are insane. No one can challenge Darius and live. I've seen it. You've seen it! We'd all be a puff of ash with a mere snap of his fingers."

"I paid the price for you. And I will keep paying it. That's all you need to know." Fully clothed, he followed me straight into the tub, burning with all he had to say. Shouting. "Hate me! Hate me with your every last thought so your father remains blind to the beautiful workings of your mind. And when it's over, I'll teach you to love me."

Practically speechless, I shook my head, water droplets falling from my hair. "It doesn't work that way. I love Ethan..."

"And we have a deal, remember that." Pressing me tight to the tiled wall, my legs slipping at odd angles due to the tub, Malcom promised, "You will have your Ethan as you submit to me. Your vow was already given. And I'll take the rest now." Mouth on mine before I might grasp the need to flee, a tangling tongue drove in.

If a kiss were life, if it were death and rebirth. If it were ownership. That was what was poured past my lips. Into me like blood. So this must be what the change felt like when a mortal was turned, the power flowing from one to another. Swelling empty veins, undoing the rot of a dead heart.

This was how a man in love kissed his bride before riding off to war.

How demons fornicated in the dark.

The very last kiss I'd survive.

I wore Malcom's ruby locked around my neck. I felt his trousers wet with suds pressed into my skin, his fingers already working between my legs. It wasn't even a question of friction or skill, it was a moment of being. One instance I was Jade, the next I was nothing.

Because I came so hard, bones broke.

The pain was unbearable, left me sobbing as I rode pure magic and disassembled.

Agony.

A zipper was torn, fingers pulled from my cunt so a ready cock might replace them. Against the wall, soaking wet and slippery. Malcom fully dressed with his slacks hanging around his thighs, he fucked me so hard the tile at my back cracked.

And I came again, clawing at his back through his sweater. Shearing the fabric when another wave of toe-curling torment broke from my center to my fingertips.

It was as if his cock were too big, the way I burned and stretched. Which was unthinkable considering the myriad lovers I'd fucked. The ways in which I'd been fucked. The amounts of cocks that had fucked me at one time.

And yet, I was overly full. When his spend began to shoot down his shaft, when even that fluid added to the corked well inside me, I burst.

Split right down the middle and shed my skin like a snake. At least that's how it felt when he cried out that he loved me.

Swallowing back screams, I found my voice didn't beg him to stop this madness. I was guilty of the opposite, I begged for more. Harder. To break me. And though he'd emptied his sack, still hard, he ravaged.

Tore at me with his teeth, drank from my breast.

Tiny flutters, minuscule pulsations came from my cunt, feathery light against the intrusion. Edging my enemy past sanity so I might know more of this pain.

"Never stop!" If he did, I'd go mad from want of it.

A world of white and blood where, for the first time in my pointless existence, I felt the truth. There was no pain in this.

Malcom only gave bliss.

18

MALCOM

She was flawless in my arms. And after the hours and myriad ways I had pleasured her, it almost seemed her blue eyes were even enthralled when they ran over the man who ruthlessly pumped his hips to fill her cunt with cock. Never had Jade looked at me in such a way. Not even when she was young, before her father poisoned her mind against me.

She had never looked at me as the females of my kind did. They begged for my body. I had been called beautiful in hundreds of languages. I had driven women to despair when I denied them.

Until that night, Jade had only seen hideousness.

For brief flickers within our joining, she saw *me*.

Inside her, moving our bodies into artistry that would make angels weep.

There was some roughness in my bed-sport. Necessary when handling a female saturated in entitlement. But should she whisper a desire, I gave.

And gave.

And took decades of yearning out upon her weaker form.

So many bites and bruises, kissed with loving lips. Healed when I put her mouth to my veins and offered power.

We drank as we fucked, her lips to the crook of my neck, mine to hers. Like husband and wife while I was cradled in her thighs. Which is what we always had been. Fate had made her mine from the day she was born.

Nipples pink, peaked, and waiting, I'd pinch, pulling them from her body until her back arched and she came... again. Full of my cock. My seed. My blood. When I moved within her, felt her velvet slickness, *I found home*. The words that fell from my lips would have shamed the long-forgotten warlord I'd been.

An eternity I'd waited for this. For slender limbs and guttural moans. For acknowledgment. For Jade to cling to me, arch her hips for what I might give. For me to show her the study I'd made of her body in all the decades I'd observed her whims.

Each nerve was attended, sometimes with pain.

Just enough to cull any thoughts she might have of retreat. The notion had crossed her mind, more than once in the hours I'd rode her hard. Small moments of conceptual duress, mental pockets still poisoned that required purging.

She'd retched once. Just the once. When I'd made her say my name. Panting from the exertion to unwork another buried layer of ugliness her father had tucked in her psyche. Fighting back, claws in my ribs, she bucked to remove me from *my home*.

My cock held fast, drilled all the harder so I might undulate my pubic bone against her sensitive and exposed clit.

"My name is Maelchon of the Picts. I've conquered and decimated tribes, countries, destroyed peoples—salted their earth while mortal. I took no wife in pillage, waiting to find you. Immortal, I waited still—slain for you, sold my soul to have and keep what's mine. The treasures I've collected, finery I've provided, your food, your drink"—pressing my lips to her gaping mouth, I breathed into her lungs—"your very air comes from me, wife."

Twisting our bodies, upending our play so my female might straddle my muscular thighs, I lifted her, lowered her, filled her up as her head lolled and her body fought through a faint. "And you will speak my old name, my true name, until I am satisfied."

But she couldn't, not with her eyes rolling back and her pussy clamping down as if to beg my sack to fill her again.

I obliged.

Convulsions moved her as if she were possessed by the devil, made all the more extravagant when my thumb mashed her clit and my hand left a bruising grip on her ass. Seated, she would stay. Forever, if I had my way.

Seated upon me. Full of me. Who loved her best and would cherish even the most horrible parts of her.

Slick with sweat, she fell forward to my chest, her hand to my heart. Little claws digging into my ribs. Like this, she slept.

Vulnerable, womb sticky with my fluids, hair matted from how I'd tangled my grip in it to hold her still when she thought to tell me how to fuck.

I had never been more in love.

Right then I made my vows, in the ancient language, inundating each word with magic. I took the vows from her as well, wove them into her being as she foolishly snored over my beating black heart.

Just as I would have stolen her from her people ages ago, taken her to my hut, and made her my wife.

Force was a powerful motivator to eternal bliss.

Vladislov kept his word to me. None interrupted.

Satan himself could be no worse than that one. But he'd been strong enough to hide portions of my memory from Darius, who never once understood how his child had lived.

In sleep, Jade's cunt tried to push me out, spilling some of my liquid gift. I'd give her more, make her fat with babies. But now my dear one needed rest. So I explored the bones of her spine, dipped my finger under her shoulder blades to work out knots. Forming her musculature into soft, pliant, comfort that made her hum in sleep.

Ethan had never done this for her. The mortal pig had never tended her.

Or given her the pleasure I had, dozens of times in the span of one night, I might add.

No male—and I had witnessed every last act of fornication my woman had endured—had made her scream as I had. While feeding, she'd only tried to kill me twice. A marked improvement and playful tussle.

Wine, food. No bath. A point had to be made when she woke. Already the sun was rising, I could feel the snapping whip of its spark upon my skin. But so full of her, I did not char. I tolerated. For as long as I might.

I sang her to deeper sleep, the old songs my mother had warbled over fires. I spoke to her what my people considered the duties of a wife. How I'd be gentle with her when I laid her in my furs. That she'd drink from none but me, growing stronger daily until she remembered all the gifts she'd been born with.

We'd have dozens of children. Mighty warriors and elegant lasses. Pureblood to glorify our house. We'd change whomever we desired, building an army of servants to tend our brood and to cook my daywalker's fine meals.

Ethan would scrub her toilet, not that I'd speak that slave's name aloud. Why disturb a perfect moment? The sun was already doing that.

My skin began to smoke, to crisp down to the bone, but I had held her in it for at least an hour. And were I not certain it would kill me and leave her without a protector, I would have lain in that misery until moonrise.

Careful with my prize, I rolled my wife from my chest, not so much as twitching when sunlight found new skin to burn. The finest sheets, wet from our lovemaking, were pulled to cover her, down-filled duvet bearing blue blossoms on a white background fell like snow over her body.

She smiled in sleep.

A thing I had never witnessed.

Warmth spread from my heart, bringing with it a horrible certainty that should I lose her, I would cease to be.

My Jade. Named for a common stone but more remarkable than a diamond.

19

I saw it, the look on her face when she woke to find her sheets smeared with char. The outline of my body where I'd burned caressing her as long as I possibly might. Fully healed and well-fed, I stood in the shadows and reveled.

Those beautiful eyes had flashed with concern. *For me.*

For a brief flicker, she'd believed I'd gone to ash in the sun. And she'd *felt*.

Sitting up, linens falling from her perfect breasts, she'd traced her fingertips over a soiled soot mark that smelled a bit of burnt flesh. Jade moved as if aching, groaning and sinking down into her sheets even as she gathered them about herself. Covering the subtle, lingering bruising I'd purposefully left behind.

I wanted her thighs to ache, her sex to throb, her joints to remember what we'd done. It was nothing that a single feed wouldn't erase. But these teachable moments were precious and never to be wasted.

"Coffee first... or a feed?" What a pushover I was. One grimace from her and I was already tripping over myself to lavish my princess with whatever she desired.

Hand to her forehead, eyes anywhere but where I lingered in the dark, she grew shy. So sweet a thing my blood-fat heartbeat. My necklace was still around her throat, had been for days, and it was there her fingers trailed next. Testing the collar, she found it was solid and not designed to be easily removed.

The fact she had not tried sooner, intriguing, though much had happened since I'd locked it around her throat.

"I've taken the liberty of filling your chests with more treasures, but that necklace will remain in place until I see fit to replace it with another." It was not about the childish way Jade enjoyed flaunting her throat before our kind, it was about ownership.

I owned her, and now she knew. Vampires did not trade flimsy rings.

She tried all the harder to remove it, but the clasp was ancient and the workings beyond her ken. "Jade, take a deep breath. Look at me."

It wasn't instant, obedience never was with her, but after a few more pants, a pouty warble, and a long sigh, she did. "Our agreement never involved this."

"You offered me your body. There was no stipulation on how often or for how long I might enjoy it. I have decided on eternity. Take better care when making deals in the future."

"Are you insane?" There it was. Her fire, her anger, her spirit. "I think you really have finally cracked. Get this damn thing off my neck."

Time wasn't wasted sauntering to her. I flashed from the dark corner to our bedside, took her wrist in hand. Her fingers flailed for a moment, the widening of her eyes betraying surprise before she tried to hide all she was feeling behind a cold mask of indifference.

"My gift to my wife stays around her pretty throat." I pressed a kiss, one that would have been considered chaste had it not lingered, to her temple. "And more gifts shall be put upon you and *inside* you."

I lowered her hand to cup my erection, Jade failing miserably at pulling away until I'd made her feel the throbbing, hard line of me. I set her free, she scooted back, the headboard containing her when I crept like a wolf over prey.

I had bathed, though I'd despised rinsing her

scent from my skin. But too much had been burnt for the perfume to remain without the stink. I had dressed: pressed slacks, cashmere sweater. Both dark and perfectly fit to my powerful form.

She'd tear at them, I was sure, when I captured her parted lips and pressed her deep into the bed where I'd finally claimed her. Patience I had in spades, but I could also be playful. I knew she secretly loved playful.

And forceful.

She loved me, she just didn't grasp it fully.

Around my tongue she garbled her complaint. "Would you stop!"

Yes. No.

Set her mouth free? Yes. Remove it from her body? No.

I tested the soft flesh above the choker, nipped hard enough she gasped. The gasp of pleasure. Unbidden, unexpected despite a full night of lessons.

"I asked you a question, wife." There was no resisting trailing my tongue over her ear. "Coffee or blood? Which would you have first?"

Petulant, fighting her response even as her nipple whorled into tight buds, my Jade said, "I don't need to feed."

"If I fuck you like this, it might hurt." She'd only get the one warning.

Though she could walk in the sun, compared to me she was fragile, and I'd left my marks in aches and pains enough. Brushing her folds, I found them wet, but she hissed. It wasn't the hiss of disgust, it was one of discomfort.

"No more."

Because I loved her, I pulled my fingers away, hovering over her to take in her routed expression. Endearingly trounced in less than five minutes. Excellent progress.

"I love you. I always have." And I'd already abstained for decades upon decades.

Her lip curled, abject perplexity smearing away her usual haughty sneer. "You say that as if it's a living thing."

Tapping my finger to my breastbone, I stated. "It is. It's here." I tapped her next. "And here." Then I looked over her skull, gave it a long stretch of contemplation. "It might take some time to undo your father's work. I'll give you patience and refrain from my stronger impulses. But I will still fuck you, and feed you, and layer you with jewels. I'll also punish and be rough with you, but I swear on all that ever is or was, that it shall only be for your own good."

"So you'll beat me when I disobey?" A fair enough question, as I'd done it before. And always to save her from her father's hand.

But there was so much more at stake than broken bones and hurt feelings. "Don't try to run. You're only safe where I can see you right now."

Sardonic, as if she'd already forgotten she was naked and I was hard, Jade said, "Going to keep me prisoner in this room?"

"No." I kissed the tip of her nose. "We're going out tonight."

She could not have been more confused when I pulled my weight away and offered her a hand to rise. "What?"

"Ethan." What magic there was in that ugly name. Her entire demeanor shifted from pliant to wary in a blink of a vampire's eye. "I thought you might want to see him."

Distrust, dislike, all the things I didn't deserve from my wife.

"We made a deal, Jade. I'll keep my end. Until it's appropriate to change him, you'll have access to see what you traded your eternity for." Catching a tangle to tuck behind her ear, I gave her the softest smile a warrior might offer.

After all, my intention was never to frighten her.

~

Jade

Malcom smiled... and it was the most chilling thing I'd ever beheld. This one had lived too long, his brains warping. He smiled at me as I fed from his wrist; me trying to keep our bodies as separated as possible before he got any ideas and began pawing between my legs again.

Scratches, gouges, throbbing bruises, and aching joins cleared up as if I'd never known pain a day in my life. Until I was sated and full and like a cat ready to nap, fat and happy.

A glass of wine was pushed between my pliant fingers, a chilled white I had not seen him procure nor smelled waiting on my nightstand. Mineral, crisp, it cleansed my palate and set me leaning back onto fluffed, char-smeared pillows. Aware I was being managed and manhandled expertly by a creature who knew me better than any other, I was at a loss.

I asked for a bath.

Immediately he denied me, Malcom looking over my healed body with a thoughtful eye. Stinking of body odor, sex, and burnt meat. Gritty and sticky and uncomfortable, I pushed past and made three steps toward my bathroom before I was flung back to the bed.

"I need to pee!"

Eyes narrowed, he hissed. "You're lying."

Yes, hissed. The same man who'd just spat all his crazy at me in the tender voice of a lover. And yes, I was lying. But I was also intensely uncomfortable with this *attention.*

A thought openly crossed his face as if something so common had never occurred to him that I was covered in soot and uncomfortable. "I'll bathe you."

I rolled my eyes.

"And after, I get to choose your clothing for our sojourn. No complaints."

This strange journey to see Ethan? Fine. Arms over my chest, I nodded.

And should have known better. Hours Malcom spent showering my body, his wet, slippery and very naked form pressed to me at all times. My hair was dried, the male working a round brush like a fucking pro. And then right there at my priceless vanity, he bent me forward and thrust in with not so much as a warning.

My cosmetics spilled, the startled scream from my lips hushed when he pressed his fingers into my mouth.

Hard, but not fast. Every thrust an exclamation point to an unspoken promise. All the while he held my eyes in the mirror, mangling my noises as fingers stroked my tongue. Massive ruby bouncing at my throat, tits vulgar in how they jiggled, all of me jerked in the tempo set upon me.

I came from penetration alone. Hard. Far too hard for so little effort on his end. My sleek, styled hair was set in disarray when he pulled out and spun me about. Jerking his fist up and down an ivory white cock that spilled pearls all over my breasts.

Belly.

My hairless mound.

I gaped when open palms rubbed it into my skin like lotion.

"Lick me clean." The statement was not a command. It was a test of the waters.

I wasn't ready for whatever it was he sought. So I shook my head no. Not even a hint of disappointment took the glow from his eyes when he praised me anyway, Malcom pumping his fist from base to tip, gathering the last drops of his cum and smearing them over the flesh of my hip.

Bodily turned around, sat back upon my vanity's seat, Malcom went back to brushing my hair, leaning down, that smile intact as he whispered, "You were wet."

20

I was dressed in white lace... the gown almost bridal. And certainly not one that came from my wardrobe. The man had shopped for me. Everything new, including the underpinnings—my preferred Agent Provocateur encasing breasts and whispering over my pussy. The shoes were blood red, glinting with stones that set off the ruby collar he'd locked around my throat. With the skirt long and clinging, there was only the vaguest flash of a glittering crimson toe when I moved, subtle and considered. This was something Malcom had spent endless hours preparing.

Bearing in mind he nightly wore the same thing in various shades of black and dark gray, I would not have expected he had it in him to adorn a woman in more than cum.

My thoughts were crude. *I was crude*. Malcom was collected to an unnatural level. None of this made sense.

"Remember, do as you will, but always where I can see you. If you cast a gate, I'll have to hurt you." He took my chin before the mirrored elevator taking us to the rooftop restaurant of the prestigious Rothschild building dinged our floor. "And I don't want to do that."

"Your threats, Malcom, are as old as you are." Eyes to my lips, a strange shiver leaving my flesh to bump, I muttered, "If there is a bridal arch and a priest on the other side of those doors, I'll set this whole building on fire."

"Very funny, Jade." His hand went to the small of my back, possessive and just a touch too low to state anything but ownership.

Doors parted, a scene so common I was already bored waiting on the other side. Humans, my humans I'd sheep-dogged over the decades having their boring political conversations, scrounging up millions, begging for scraps while wearing Armani. And into an apparent fundraiser for Senator Parker we strolled.

Noticed.

Immediately noticed.

For I had been away for over a week, no Ethan on my arm, arriving with a stranger far more beautiful than any living creature. One who made it very clear that he was not there with me, but that I was there with him.

He might as well have pissed all over me the way he glared around the room. *Mine. Do not touch.*

It didn't move the humans as it should have. Already the senator descended down upon me, frown fixed above his sagging chin. "You'll arrange a private chat between me and your father. Technicalities are to be ironed out."

I'm not sure why it came over me then, but I was so utterly weary of all of this—these people, their politics, the human idea of wealth. "Let me guess, no check arrived. Short of funds?"

Never had I spoken with such rudeness to this man. I'd always groveled, and bantered, and submitted to grotesque jokes and a *woman's place*.

The senator's face went purple, his voice dropping low as if to prevent a further scene. "If this is due to my nephew's liaison, I can assure you she'll be kept out of sight."

Not removed from the equation, but tucked away so as to save me further embarrassment. "And the baby?"

I don't know why I said it, why I dug that dagger in specifically to cause Ethan harm. Because there was no way either the senator or Ethan's illustrious father knew of the fetus. A child I had just done harm by making it real with words.

Calculations, considerations of the most unconservative kind worked the wheels in the old republican's skull. Was it too late for abortion? Could the baby be given away? How much was this going to cost to hide from the tabloids? "Will be sent abroad to school, of course."

I really was evil... "Of course."

Before the strangest wave of self-reproach might mingle with the unhealed ache in my heart, I heard my name called. With joy. As if the world once again turned because I'd been found. "Jade!"

Ethan was there, as promised, sauntering over in a ten-thousand-dollar suit. No pregnant blonde beauty at his side. Careful of my red lipstick, he kissed my cheeks in the European style, took my fingers and asked me if I'd care for a drink, already pulling me toward the bar.

Leaving the senator alone with Malcom, who was infinitely dangerous and smiling again.

"Listen, I know I should have called." Running a hand through his golden hair, mussing it perfectly, Ethan gave a self-deprecating grin. "You just threw me out... and I... I you know."

"Left me for another woman."

"Well"—he stood a bit taller, slightly put out

—"I didn't leave. You had me removed from our house."

"*My house*, where your girlfriend had been living without my knowledge." And one thing bothered me above all others. "She wore my things."

That brought out a grin. "You're the same size."

I didn't even know how to respond to this, it was like speaking to a happy monkey that had no concept of right or wrong. And considering who I was, all the atrocious things I'd done, I was a bit shaken. "Ethan, apologize this instant."

And he did, with great big, wide, shining eyes. "I'm sorry, Jade."

"Do you love me?"

"Of course I do!" This exclamation came with an enthusiastic kiss that felt more for show than real. Because Ethan knew never to kiss lips painted blood red. Not unless he had a chance to repair his appearance or was giving me a gift draped in diamonds. "These situations, they're nothing to people like us. I'll tuck her away, you'll never need to see her again. Split my time between you. Of course, she'll never be"—he waved his hands around the grandeur and elite gathered sipping their martinis—"a part of this."

Oh, the foolish boy. Malcom was going to give this to me. He was going to give me this bumbling, stupid, sweet idiot. And there would be no need for mistresses or hidden families. We weren't the fucking Kennedys, and I had no need to tolerate a Marilyn. He'd be changed and mine forever, and all I had to do was let Malcom fuck me.

Like he had already done a dozen times.

My cheeks grew flushed, my breath uneven, and without intent my eyes sought him across the crowd. Watching me. One glance, and I knew he knew.

I was thinking of him fucking me right now.

Which was so beyond disturbing that I blanked completely. Ignoring Ethan sputtering on about our future, his less than subtle hints that I better get those funds to his uncle before he addressed my father directly.

Wait.

Had Ethan just threatened me?

Had *my* Ethan dared, considering his sins? I knew my eyes went red as disgusting human blood, redder than the ruby at my throat. And all the anger that I hadn't had a chance to purge because I'd been too busy mourning left me looking much less than human.

A thing witnessed by a powerful family's golden child and black sheep.

It was utterly cliché, laughable, but undeniably right in that moment. "Do you have any idea who my father is? Can you grasp what he would fucking do to your entire family for disturbing him for even a moment? He'd see you all slaughtered and walk away laughing."

Ethan went white. The pallor worn by all humans trapped as livestock in the Cathedral.

"You want money, power, things I have assured for your family for an age? The sacrifices I've made to guarantee a Parker holds the Senate? The bailouts for your father's empire? Tell me again that I'd be wise to make my expected donation to a political campaign that goes against your family's direct orders."

"Jade?" I was scaring him.

It felt wickedly good and equally awful. "Open borders, Parker. I don't give a fuck how the senator sells it. Your family works for your bread like everyone else."

A cool hand came to my back, instantly smoothing raised hackles. "I think it might be time to leave, my love."

A blink. Just one, and red went to blue; fangs retracting. I had not even realized I'd gone so far.

"Idiot human"—Malcom stood between us, only inches left between my Ethan and my guardian—"you will remember nothing of this except that you're sorry for rudely asking your ex-girlfriend for a political donation. Which she denied. Bad form."

And off I was swept, through the party, and into the elevator, not twenty minutes after I had arrived.

In a daze, I confessed, "I don't know what came over me…"

All I could see was my smeared red lipstick reflected back to me from the polished elevator doors, and I was annoyed. Annoyed Ethan had ruined it.

He'd ruined everything.

21

Maybe I was young, inexperienced in real feeling. Maybe Gerard wasn't real. Try as I might in those awful moments in the elevator, I couldn't remember how much I'd love Ethan's grandfather.

Or... I remembered someone. But it wasn't the long-lost previous version of Ethan I still pined for.

And my father had most likely done this to me. For sport maybe. To keep me complacent and sad, and hating the world for taking what I'd loved. But I was starting to think that I had never loved. That I was a pretty shell, a puppet, and a dupe so unworthy even Ethan Parker chose another over me.

Silent tears smeared my smoky eye and mascara, though my expression hardened as I considered.

What if nothing about me was real? What if

everything, every part of what made me *me* was all made up by dear old dad?

"It won't be easy." Warm palm still resting at the dip of my back, Malcom thought to soothe me with a simple gesture.

Blue eyes, then red, then blue. Red again. I could not control what was churning in my scarred and broken brain. "I think I died that day, when my brain fell on the floor. Whatever I am now, I'm not that girl in the blue dress who ate her cat on accident."

Reaching forward, Malcom pressed the hold button, stopping our descent. In a mirror-lined box where I could see myself from every angle, where I saw infinite facsimiles of myself and this male, he took my hand. Played with my fingers as if touching me in such a way were novel, exciting, that it *soothed* him. "You are capable of overcoming and thinking for yourself. Of growing up, of choosing to resist what you think you know and what you are afraid you know."

Because I needed to hear Malcom say it again, I looked him dead in the eye. "Gerard was never real?"

"Not the version of him you cling to. And yes, I did have him shipped out to fight in the war despite his family's attempts to keep him out of battle."

"So my father didn't lie when he told me Gerard

never loved me..."

Malcom shook his head.

"What's real? What isn't real?" Breaking our stare, I looked at myself in those mirrors, at the long line of my face and back, over and over into infinity. "How many times have I figured this out?"

"You've come close, but never this close."

Because Darius would have caught wind that his wind-up toy needed a tune up. What he'd do to me after this. What he'd tear and replace and rework... "I won't go back to the Cathedral."

"Listen to me, Jade." Pulled forward into a cool embrace, touched in a way I think I'd been manipulated into seeing only with disgust, I tolerated and tested the waters as Malcom spoke. "Help me place Vladislov on the throne and all of us will be free."

"And what makes you think he'd be any better than the devil we know?"

"Does it matter?" A hand cupped my cheek, pressing my face to his chest. An act so intimate and uncomfortable that I knew it was my father's exploitation in my mind that made me cringe so. "He has his own agenda that has little to do with you."

"Which would be?"

Strict as he'd always been with me, Malcom pulled back enough so that I might see his smirk. "None of your business."

"Would I still have to"—I gesture upward to where the fundraiser continued—"do this? Let them fuck me? The quota?"

"No." The resonance of his denial, of the rage I glimpsed in that simple answer. It made me nervous that it was all too good to be true.

So I tested Malcom, because nothing in my world, it seemed, could be real or trusted. "You'll still give me Ethan."

Glittering eyes flashed, more agitation of a different kind. "That was our agreement."

I cocked an eyebrow. "Can you make him love me?"

"Yes."

And I wanted that, I wanted that love I'd thought I'd had. That playful sort and laughter, the days in bed where he took pleasure of himself in my body. Like a drug. An impulse I couldn't trust but needed to feed. "When?"

"And you can do as you wish with him, sweet Jade. That fool mortal or immortal is of no consequence to me. Our housecat, one you can fuck if you feel the need to purge that desire."

And right there I grasped that Malcom understood exactly what was wrong with me. That after a lifetime of witnessing my rewrites, he knew me in a way I'd never possibly know myself.

The feeling, like most feelings these days, was unsettling. But it was also sanctuary.

"Who would I have been if..." Darius had not been my father.

Gentle, he tucked my hair behind my ear, massaging the lobe as he smiled. "A spoiled, rotten brat. Too beautiful for her own good and impossibly stubborn."

I smirked and Malcom's response was instant, brighter than any sun, and overwhelming. He kissed me.

Tongue tracing my lips so I might part them, fingers delving into my hair, Malcom took of that small smile, feasted on it, groaning into my open mouth. "Tell me, Jade, that you understand what this is."

A collar around my neck, a white dress, a pet, the touch of a starved man already bunching my skirt up and unzipping his fly. Right there in the elevator. He'd already had me before the soiree, he'd had me dozens of times the evening prior. Insatiable. A word I'd never have considered applying to Malcom. But one second I was breathing out a response, the next he was inside me.

Full.

I don't know why out of all the cocks I'd ever choked with my cunt, his felt so very different. Breath stolen, jerking from the frantic way he worked to bury himself deeper, and clung. It was either that or fall spiraling backward into the abyss.

"Tell me!" He panted at my ear.

He hit a spot inside me that was tender yet eager to know friction. When I squealed and hiked my leg higher, Malcom was not appeased. Not when he wanted words.

"Tell me, or I'll take it, and I won't even give you the ghost of a choice." Why was he doing this to me, here, where I could not control the pitch of my moans and was ashamed? This wasn't like fucking Ethan in all the dirty ways and silly places. Here, I wasn't in ultimate control.

In fact, I had none.

At all.

Not over my own body's reactions to a throbbing, glorious shaft. Not to my mental state, which grew more precarious by the minute. Not over my future.

This man had taken it regardless of what I might be underneath my father's influence. He'd called me wife, borne my teasing because it was nothing to him. Because there was no undoing it no matter if I agreed, disagreed, desired another, or wanted none at all.

And I was coming, and rabid, head thrown back to cry out like a beast.

"It's the end of me." I'd said, breath lost in the

waves of saturating, perfect pleasure that was so far beyond sex I didn't understand up from down.

Filled, fluttering and clenching with every bit of unnatural strength my pussy possessed, I milked his cum, sucked it from him. Felt each burst run from the grinding base of his cock to the uncut head.

My body seemed hungry for him, for a chance to be what it was without holding back for fear of breaking a fragile human. And I'd never climaxed with a vampire before Malcom—unless I'd been in the feed and too consumed to consider something as inconsequential as sperm.

It was over almost as quickly as it had begun, but no less earth-shattering.

With so many mirrors, it was impossible to miss that I looked truly fucked… and not just physically.

After smoothing down my skirt, pocketing panties I didn't even know he'd torn, Malcom took my chin and made a clear, concise demand. "Lick me clean."

This was no test.

Mascara having run down my cheeks, hair mussed, dress half here and half there, I looked every bit the prostitute I'd played for years. But I knelt, holding his eyes, lost utterly, and took him in my mouth as a wife.

∼

THE ELEVATOR MOVED, the door opened, and I strolled into the lobby on the arm of a well-satisfied male. With the flavor of his cum on my tongue, I followed along, a bit dazed, my thoughts stuck on the fact he tasted different than a human.

Less bleachy. Salty, but also almost radiant like blood. Which had drawn down my fangs once he'd popped from my mouth, because I'd wanted more. Tempted to reach under my skirt and gather what ran down my thighs, but somewhat humiliated over the thought.

Because it wasn't a sex game where I'd lick my fingers to entice him, it was *hunger*. Groaning I'd forced my eyes from his swollen member, already having sucked the entire thing down my throat, to 'lick clean' until it was only my spit that shined the fat head peeking from his foreskin. I'd wanted to nibble there, to play and rub at him. To see what made his knees weak and what made him hiss frustration.

Cocks could be such fun things.

I also wanted to sink my teeth into that perfect vein running down his turgid length and drain him until he'd be too weak to fight me. At that thought, I'd known Malcom would have allowed it, because we both knew he'd overpower me no matter how I might gorge.

And I found the idea somewhat exciting, my

cheeks going pink. Still on my knees before him, but looking to the floor.

No mirrors, no male. Only his leg and a polished shoe that I could ignore. Until he'd put his hand to my hair, told me he loved me, and that I'd earned a great reward. That he was proud of me. That he'd never witnessed in all his years of endless life such a survivor. That I would give him fine sons and deadly daughters.

Slouched and mixed up, I listened, fought back my outrageous hunger, and thought I might have found a piece of myself there on the floor of that elevator.

Malcom helped me rise before the door might open and I'd be seen in such a state. He smoothed my dress and wiped the black tearstains from my cheeks, his fingertip tracing the line of my lips to tidy smeared crimson gloss.

With the practiced grace of a gentleman, the ancient warlord led me through the building's foyer and out into the night. But I knew Malcom. He was no gentleman. Gentlemen didn't gain the rank he had in my father's court. They didn't fuck like he did.

They didn't plan to betray their king and steal the princess for themselves.

22

MALCOM

She could not resist cutting glances at me. Or working her throat. I could see her swallowing, knew her tongue toyed with the tips of her fangs the way freshly-changed vampires marveled at their new weapons.

It was a tick, something again to remind me of just how young my bride was. How much she needed me.

There was a reason all freshly-turned served three hundred years of service in this new world. And Jade, as royalty, had only ever been served. Not that she had not been a slave the whole time... but she'd had no master to guide her. To teach her beyond what I might *suggest* as her guardian, custodian, and chaperon. But those days were over. I'd take my hand to her backside if that's what it took to help her bloom.

I was her husband in all ways that mattered. My sperm swam through her belly even now, and would nightly for the rest of eternity. I'd lavish her with much more than jewels. She'd know the true attention of a powerful being. One who truly loved her.

One who would continue to keep her in line.

An adorable grumble came from her stomach, Jade pretending as if nothing had happened.

"Already hungry?" I teased, warmth spreading through my gaze in equal measure with gentle mockery.

She was. Her cold-eyed glance could never lie, not to me. Embarrassed, she chose her typical silence. But like a true fresh-turned, accidently eyed my throat. So much for the daywalker who'd starved herself and only dined once a week.

Had I the power to break her of that habit fifty years ago...

But her fucking father. As much as I loved Jade, I hated him. And I would see him cut asunder, scorched, his limbs spread across the world to never reunite. I'd see his dust, swallow it in my wine.

"Tonight we return to the Cathedral. You will feed, rest, and be unmolested."

"I've never left this city." Jade thought she was

clever, evasive with such a comment. She was cute, extremely ruffled and ready to run.

Tightening my arm where hers was looped with mine, I made it so not only could she not pull away, she could not accidentally cast a gate without taking me with her.

She noted the aggression, digging in her heels and looking every last bit betrayed. "I'm not going back there."

"Soon I'll take you to Paris, to Dubrovnik, to all the wonders of Europe so you might play and leave this city for the first time in your life. I'll spoil you with feasts crafted by master chefs, with rare wine and rarer jewels."

"You listen to me, Malcom." The hissing, the biting, and the scratching were soon to begin—as if her sweet fangs or tiny claws could possibly do me any damage. "I will not go back."

"And where would you run? Our apartment? Another country? Into enemy territory as a physically weak but highly desired daywalker? I'd find you in minutes. I can feel where you are with every pulse of my heart. And if another beat me to you, an ancient older than your father, what then? Would you rather be devoured so an old corpse might feel the sun one last time? Or will you trust me?"

Her eyes, makeup already smeared, watered. Her beautiful bitten lip shook. "Is this some kind of game to you? Is that what you do? You and my father? Do you toy with my memories until I unravel then take me back home for a proper whipping and a purged mind?"

Out in the open, where we could be heard and might be, I cupped her cheek and asked her to be braver. I reminded her that she was the daughter of a veritable demon and capable of so much more than either of us might imagine.

And I made her a promise. "Vladislov."

"What?" Impatient, her heart beating fast enough to send a human into a stroke, Jade's chest rose and fell. All of her looked ill. "That means nothing to me."

"Do as he asks, when he asks it. It could be that easy."

"And he'll kill my father?" I'd pushed her too far, Jade throwing up the hand that wasn't trapped by my arm. "You're all insane. No one can best him. You've seen what he can do. The entirety of his body can spread out to all corners of a room. All corners of your mind. He is the devil, and you are a fool for thinking your foreigner might actually take his throne. I'm going to run!"

With a sigh, and a heavy heart, I caught her flailing arm and kissed her knuckles despite how she fought. "Then I'm going to have to chain you."

"You wouldn't dare!"

But we were already falling through a gate. One expertly crafted to deliver us outside Jade's preferred entrance to the Cathedral.

My hand over her shrieking mouth, I dragged her through a foyer with a new, head-shaking, eye-rolling vampire who must have heard how difficult and obstinate the king's daughter could be. Not a soul stopped me. No matter how she kicked, tore at my palm, and tried to scream for freedom.

Spectators, witnesses, smirking lips and the old dame's style of waving hand. They had seen this before: they found it boring; they found it titillating; they found it nothing. In this dead kingdom of lost souls and the damned.

I wasted no time dragging my cargo to the conservatory, even less parting the doors and forcing her inside. Then they were dragged closed despite her attempts to pull them back open. Barred, with steel.

To the guards, I said. "No one enters. Ignore her raving and lies. The princess is in one of her moods."

And I left her there.

Already aware a fine dinner of extremely rare Kobe beef, properly prepared as it would have been in the Land of the Rising Sun, waited under a dome. Two bottles of fragrant wine also sat atop her table.

One red, decanted and perfect. The second white, chilled yet uncorked.

She'd had blood enough from me earlier to tolerate a day or two while I did the work deserving of our house.

Though I couldn't hear her while I went about my night, I knew she cried. I suffered with her, and took out my frustration on my food. Not that I killed any of the well-fed and well-bred humans from my personal stock. I just took a bit more, a touch roughly, and didn't give a shit that they begged for mercy.

Of all immortals in this kingdom, there were few more merciful than I.

Then a hunt began, the dregs in the lowest pens released for sport. In that game I was savage, collecting the most ears with ease. Vladislov, still the guest of King Darius, found the whole thing hilarious.

Jade

Days before, I'd accidentally cast a gate while in the throes of unwanted orgasm, I'd dropped my sad self into the throne room before my personal Jesus

Christ. But now, stuck in my conservatory I could do nothing. Try as I might.

Blood ran down my nose, an aneurysm to be sure, I'd tried so hard.

And when I could not find my exit from hell, I made hell my plaything. Everything I might reach I destroyed. The glass coffin of my childhood, trinkets, baubles, priceless art, bedding, the rug. I even pulled every last settee and couch asunder. Raging like a demon.

Red eyes, sharp fangs.

Powerless.

Malcom would pay for this. Trickery, mockery, *lies*. He would pay when I tore his cock off with my teeth and shoved it so far up his ass a creature incapable of shitting would never be able to get it out.

Of course, he'd grow a new dick. Leaving me more than happy to repeat the procedure.

The pain I would bring down upon that man. The *hate* I felt. Like a warm blanket, reassuring and normal. Wrapped in the cocoon of loathing, covered in down feathers from torn blankets, I made a nest in shattered glass and pulled my knees to my chin.

I slept through the worst of the sun, waking at dusk.

There was no water waiting when I woke.

I, the princess of this kingdom, was made to

stand, burned as I was, and walk to my bathroom to drink from the tap.

Scooping water into my palm, sucking it down a dry throat, I died a little more. Until I stood straight and saw myself in the cracked remains of the mirror. A horror.

A demon's spawn.

In great need of a shower, a new life, a rebirth.

Poisoned by this place and the horrible creatures gathered in it.

Envy at a memory, one my father would tear from my mind the second he sensed it, lanced my being. Vladislov sitting daddy's throne. How I would have loved, even in play to have sat that throne.

To have the immortals here look upon me with veneration. Instead, I'd been dragged inside screaming, not for the first time, and laughed at. The tittle-tattle most likely carrying on would leave me shamed for years.

I'd sucked that bastard's cock down my throat, choked on it—gagging and drooling the way men preferred.

"Jade."

Hands to my marble bathroom vanity, burning as if the fires of hell had been born in my womb, I refused to look toward the one who had reduced me so low. "Get out."

But Vladislov was not moved by something as pathetic as I. "Come, love. We'll find a place in your *palace* to talk."

It was then I realized sunlight drenched us both, the remainder of the day. A pink sky. Death to any vampiric immortal.

"Come, child," he murmured to me. Beautifully ugly. That long, waved brown hair shining and glorious. "You've had your tantrum. Let it be done."

My clothing was shambles, my skin left with marks of broken things and self-harm. Still I turned to face my savior. "Can you really steal the throne from Satan?"

"Let's talk of the River Seine. And beautiful things."

The melody of his song, the very look he laid upon me. My own father had never looked at me in such a way. "I would have been a good daughter…"

How he dug in so deep with so little effort. "I know, child."

"You asked before if I would burn the Cathedral with everyone inside."

"And?"

"I like Marie. She's always been kinder to me than the others." My forehead softened, my lips growing lax. "Perhaps it is her Hapsburg jaw and lack of 'immortal' beauty. Or the fact she lost so many babies when her kingdom fell. She was the first to ever offer me cake. Did you know that?" Brushing rooted glass from my forearm, I continued. "I don't think anyone does. Something so inconsequential wouldn't even have interested my father."

Footstep cracking more broken glass under his heel, Vladislov dared come nearer. "And did you care for the cake?"

"I devoured the attention. Sitting on her lap like a prized poodle."

"You're lonely."

"Yes." None could be more lonely than I.

With a wink, something evil professed. "No fire then. The only friends you've ever known are here, terrible as they are."

Enough. I'd had enough of being toyed with on all fronts. "You said we were going to talk of the Seine."

He moved with the same speed as my daddy. There one instant, in another before one might see. Picking a feather from my hair, Vladislov blew on it to make it fly away. Together we watched the bit of down tumble and float, to land in the chaos. And then silence.

Which fed me.

This man, this thing who could tolerate just a touch of dying light, grasped me by the soul.

Glancing up from the wreckage on the ground, I

caught his eyes, daring much in my request. "I'm hungry."

He grinned. "Don't be greedy."

Yet still he offered me his wrist.

It was like drinking ebony. Glassy warm and blacker than pitch.

23

Telling someone as spoiled and rotten and twisted as I not to be greedy, was, in itself, silly. Even at my age, I was incapable of being anything but. Lips to skin that felt like dry paper, cautious in how I punctured, and feeling the strangest itch upon the parts of my skull that had been put back together, I sank in my fangs.

Delicately.

Like a lady sipping port, pinky up.

Rapture hit me harder than my brains had hit that wall years ago. It took me by the throat, stole my soul from right out of my body, and had me tearing my lips away before more than a few drops of infinite darkness smeared my tongue.

I could not have been greedy if I'd wanted to! To drink of that man would kill me.

"Sure you've had enough, child?" He made a show of rolling up his sleeve, exposing the veins in his strong forearms and tan skin.

He stood in the last of the day's dredge of sun, had entered my pretty prison without effort, had offered me the taste of infinity. Did my father's blood hold eons like this? How had I survived drinking from this man as a child? "What are you?"

"I am whatever I want to be." He cut me a secretive smirk, teasing, playful even. "Old, to be sure."

Wiping my lips as if some of that dreadful perfection might still linger there, I spoke plainly. Because there was absolutely no point in prevaricating with this one. "The older they get, the more their minds warp. What's to make you any different than him should you take his throne?"

He cocked a brow. "Nothing at all."

"I'm less than one hundred but I feel ten thousand." I felt older than any river he might want to discuss.

"Yet you act like you're five."

True. I was aware of my faults. More aware by the minute, blockages in my mind easing until the overspill of ugliness behind them left me reeling. "I think I might *need* another drink."

If just a few drops of him had untangled hints of what was hidden in me, a mouthful might give me back what I lost that day my brains hit the floor.

"By all means." The same wrist was offered, the greedy girl I was nervous to so much as scratch his skin.

My lips hovered there, amidst the wreckage of my tantrum, and mental scar tissue snapped apart and made me hate myself more.

I remembered so many disgusting things I'd done. And considering what I'd recalled before, felt so dirty in my flesh that I wished the fading sun would literally burn it all away. Breathing over his skin, over that wrist filled with truths and punishment, I fell to my knees.

They were cut apart on shards of glass, the pain welcome and not nearly enough. "I've destroyed families. I've rewritten histories, done terrible things... because I loved my father and craved his love in return."

As if he were some ancient saint and I a supplicant, he put a hand to my head. "Do you not want your mother's love?"

No. "My mother is dead. I doubt she had much love for me when I ripped my way out of her body."

"What a sad tale..." Said with what felt like real remorse. Ancients couldn't feel *real* anything. He pressed his wrist closer to my hovering mouth. Offering another taste.

And I was too young to know better. "The more of me you undo, the uglier my life will be. You should have just left me alone." Yet still I sunk my teeth in.

And unlike that first sip, I drank.

Remembering rapes, sodomy, prostitution, the ways in which my father had sold me for whatever gain he might. Tears when it hurt, until it didn't hurt. Until it didn't feel like anything. Until I was fucked like a robot, or bent over and took it like a cow might take a bull—chewing cud and bored in my field.

I don't know why it was the sex that broke through first. Perhaps because under my father's influence, it bothered me the most. I was a dishtowel, a tissue used and discarded. Nothing more than a thing to wipe fluids on and cast to the floor.

What search was there for a grandchild in this? This lazy approach of bending my body to every immortal male's whims.

Two thrusts had come from Malcom as I'd bent over that table while my father had watched. I'd been physically ill afterward. Two thrusts after my sire had left the room and Malcom, the first ever, asked me if I wanted him to stop.

And he had. Just like that. No complaints. No violence.

Instead, he'd tried to comfort me as I cursed his cock and threatened his life.

For the life of me, I couldn't understand why the

idiot might think he loved me. I was not worth loving. Perhaps age had made him as mad as the man whose black blood trickled like sludge down my throat. This man who had physically pieced my skull back together ages ago, who now mentally ripped through so much damage I'd never be the same.

Never.

The scar tissue was still there, I was just aware of it now. And in many cases could see exactly what was hidden within its knots and gnarls.

And the lies... the untruths planted to make me compliant. Losing those stopped my heart.

Because I knew the answer the rest of the flock would give, I broke suction from that vein of death, and looked up at the smiling figure before me. "Do you find this all amusing?"

"When I made your father, I knew he'd do great things. Build empires. Slaughter enemies." Soft, manicured fingers ran through my hair. "But you might be his greatest accomplishment."

It was just the type of lie that fed me more deeply than any blood might. How I craved acceptance. How it had made me tolerate hell for another taste.

"You won't be a good king. Not if you created Darius and let him run wild for thousands of years." It had to be said. "You don't care."

"Can a father not love his son despite his... shortcomings?" The tip of a finger tapped my nose. "Can he not love his granddaughter?"

I was not falling for it. Not again. "You only saved me because Malcom traded eternal fealty. Otherwise I would have dragged myself to my death, alone, scared, and missing half my brain!"

"We could debate why I was where I was when your lover found me and fell to his knees. I could spin tales more beautiful than any your father planted in your mind. But to be true, I can't recall exactly why I walked where I walked that day. There is something else here that draws my thoughts. Something I want but can't find."

Negotiation, politics, and plain demands. This was my safe space. This was comfortable. So I rose from the ground, bloody knees ignored, and asked point-blank what the sire of my father could possibly lack.

All I received for an answer was a kiss on the cheek. And then he was gone, right as the sun vanished and night broke in.

For two more days I was kept locked in my rooms, living in a new mind that felt alien and too large. For two days I tidied my mess. Piling up broken, glittering things. Sweeping them with the remains of my ruined wardrobe.

There was more chaos than clean. But some

parts of my tiled floors did sparkle as if freshly polished. The rest were cracked, broken, and in need of replacing. I slept, and I dreamed, and I drank more water from the tap. And as the hours crept on, as the sun rose and set, I found that tap water tasted better than any blood I'd ever known.

Malcom came on the third night bearing food. I refused his wrist, eating chicken wings off the bone and chugging a local, frothy beer, and found I liked both things.

Heaven help him, he tried to talk to me, but I wasn't ready. It wasn't stubbornness, not at its heart. It was something unnamable. I had almost a century to process and only a handful of hours in which I'd been able to do it.

I thought of the Seine. A river I'd only seen in pictures and how Vladislov had tempted me with the idea of it. I thought of Paris, and art, and modern women, and food.

I thought of what real love might feel like, staring at the male who believed in his heart he felt that emotion for me.

Puzzling over this concept as I sucked the marrow from the bones. *Staring* at Malcom, at a man beautiful beyond description and devious as my devil of a father, I thought long and hard over the mechanics of it.

And wasn't sure our kind was capable of such a human thing.

"You have permission to fuck me, if you want to." That was all I said to him over that dinner of peasant food and beer.

It earned a sad smile, one from a man who just might know the exact torture of a broken heart. "Not tonight, my love."

24

MALCOM

The state of her rooms was a reflection of the state of her mind. Piles of shattered things, spots she'd cleared, everything sharp and ready to harm her—her glass cage where my beautiful bird could never sing.

In all my centuries, I'd never seen a being look so sad. Not even the humans kept by the worst vampire houses. Not even the cattle who'd lost everything only to live out their remaining days drained of the last drop of blood in their veins. Until withered and unwanted, burned where thousands of others just as unwanted as they had been sent to burn.

Ash that floated over a polluted city, forgotten, mourned... nothing.

"You're thinking to yourself right now how

anyone could love you." And I didn't understand how it was possible, but I loved her even more in that moment. To the point I thought my heart might burst and the soul I'd sold was returned to me.

She didn't answer or shrug, just watched me. Waiting for some trick, that little girl in a blue dress all grown up. There was no minute flinch when I took her hand. A first. Rubbing warmth into her fingers, I relished this intimacy. I took things slowly with my virgin.

That's what she was now, reborn. Jaded, and aptly named.

Paying strict attention, I smoothed each of her fingers from base to tip, gently attended the webbing between them, before turning her palm up, to spread that flesh with my thumbs. My flower melted, just a little of that ice she'd been encased in from birth seeping away from simple kindness.

"You are not what he made you to do, or the traits he coerced you to embrace. I have always seen the real you. I see it now. And someday, you will too." I pressed a kiss to that palm, and felt a tear fall from my cheek to drip down her wrist. I, the old, tried warrior, wept for this damaged thing that was beyond dear to me.

And by her sudden, violent retreat, I think it might have frightened her more than any torment her father might bring down upon us should he discover we even shared such a conversation. Hand to her heart, fingers fluttering, lips thin, cheeks white, eyes wide. She gave an inch, even as she took another step away.

Rising so she'd be forced to see all of me—my stature, my strength, my prowess, and my superiority to other males, I declared, "I do love you. Every single thing about you. I always have."

"I'm grotesque." This she said, looking down at her body as if all she saw was rotting flesh and bloated limbs.

I flashed to her side, took her fingers again, and kissed the tips. "But there you're wrong. You're clean. Brand new. Mine to treasure."

Challenging, because she was born royal and would never easily cede, Jade sneered. "How do you know that you don't just love me because Darius made you? How do you know it's real? I've had my thoughts ripped apart for the last few days, and let me tell you, most of what is trapped in my skull is utter bullshit. It's no different for anyone else in this place."

This was the question I had been pining for. "Because your bastard of a father tried repeatedly to take it away from me. *And every single time he failed.* I'm far older than you, I know how to maneuver in ways you're too impatient to grasp. I know my love is real because he forbade me from ever telling you how much I cared. Forbade me to woo you, to be kind to you, to even touch you unless it was to draw your ire." I pinched a strand of her hair, the way I had for ages. The way that always pissed her off. Only this time, she looked down at my fingers and saw what they were about. "All he could do was forbid. Take small moments from my memory... but they always grew back. They grew back because since I held you in my arms, all I've ever thought of was how to love you best."

Narrowing her eyes, it looked as if she'd react as she had thousands of times in the past to my touch. Shove me away and hiss that I was beneath her notice.

But that wounded bird resisted, fighting the urge so hard her eyes closed from the effort. Brow tight, several deep breaths expanded her chest. More of my fingers stroking her hair, pushing her to try.

She whispered, "Vladislov is far worse than my father. Do you grasp that?"

"I think you misunderstand him."

"*I drank from him.* I saw what he was." Eyes opening, she gave me a look. A look that spoke more than the words that followed it. "He stood with me in the sun."

Ancients were different than other immortals. God-like, and necessary to keep our numbers in check. To rule hordes of bloodthirsty beasts. And one day both Jade and I would stand amongst them. We too would be changed by time, altered, blood black as death. But we would do it together, whole of mind, and sound of heart. The same soul, in two separate bodies, reunited.

Fated.

The reason I never took another wife. No female flesh as spoils of war.

I had recognized her from the moment she'd been delivered into my arms. And should I die, I would be reborn to find her again. For eternity. Over, and over.

Because there was no such thing as heaven or hell. This I knew. There was only with or without one's soulmate.

But she was too stuck on other issues for me to breach such a weighty subject. "It doesn't matter what he is. What matters is what we have." I needed her to understand that the trivialities, the cost to be together, was nothing. I'd destroy entire countries, burn them and all living things in their borders, laughing, if that's what I had to do so I might claim this female. "Your father envies me for what I achieved in finding you. Vladislov envies just the same. All those doomed to endless life who have not discovered their other half covet this, whether they know it or not. Recognize what is before you and forget the rest. It could be so easy, Jade."

So easy to just sweep her into my arms and carry her off to the place I had prepared. Lock her away from all things dangerous, where she would be only mine until she grew stronger. Until she understood and accepted what this was.

"You're not listening to me!" A sigh, one heavy with frustration, and she swatted my hand from her hair. "Talk of love, if you want to. Talk of"—she gestured between us before she began to pace—"all of this. But you're ignoring my point because you know I'm right. That creature will eat us on a whim."

Her panic was... unfortunate. I'd hoped these days might have cleared her head. "He and I have an arrangement."

"He created my father." The confession spoken with awe and terror.

That I had not known, though such knowledge only gave me faith that soon all I had sacrificed and all my darling had suffered would reap us the ultimate reward. So I got to my knees before this woman, and startled her all the more.

Before she might dart back, I took her hips in my hand. Held her before me as I groveled for her love—for more effort from my lady, even though I know she suffered. "And your father made you.

Once a toddler who could cast gates without chanting, so powerful in magic that he fractured her mind so she might never move against him. Darius wants you to think as little of yourself as possible. Degraded you into dust. I did all I could to shield you; though it might not have always appeared that way, I did. And I have gathered such splendors to please you. Every desire that's truly *yours*, I can fulfill."

"You're a little bit insane. You know that right?" Wiping her eyes with the back of her hands, she gave me a look of pity. "Neither of us will survive whatever game Vladislov plays."

From across the room came an overly gentle, "You may call me Grandfather."

She screamed, jumped right out of my hands, portal and all. To appear twenty feet away. Tottering on her feet, unsure how she did it, Jade fell flat on her ass into one of her piles of my broken gifts.

And there she cried like a baby. Mind a ruin, body abused for so long she couldn't differentiate what was her choice from what wasn't, and in pain. When I stepped forward to go to her, to try again to explain, Vladislov appeared from the shadows and held up his hand.

Eternal fealty. I had to obey.

So that entity—that creator of great, evil things

—went to her instead. Crouching down, wiping her tears, and whispering things I'd never know.

I'd never know them because part of our arrangement was that I could never ask. And Jade, she never offered information. What I'd pulled from her over the years, was taken by force.

But my lady calmed: the type of forced calm minutes away from violence. A kind of violence that came from desperation should the beast who had cornered her make one wrong move. The kind of violence that would see her ended. Wounded rabbit, rabid wolf.

For this woman, I was not above begging. "Please, don't hurt her."

"She…" The man's long, thin fingers, stroked her wet cheek. "She is my family. Are you not, child? If I let your daddy run wild for eons, why would I tarnish this precious flower?"

"Please," I said again. Darius knew sweet words too. Darius had learned them from him.

And I had bet our entire futures on the whims of a God.

"I cannot recall the last time I offered someone succor." And how chilling such a phrase could be from something so powerful.

For he had not offered it to little Jade. I had paid for it. But now he looked amused, long hair draped over his shoulder and waved, impeccably combed, just like the rest of him. A fancy man for all his less desirable features.

The being came to a decision. "If she'll drink once more, I'll leave her be. Comfort your wife and tell her to open her jaw."

It was there I saw how he'd already tried to tempt her, a wrist offered, the same wrist he'd fed her from the night she'd been left in pieces. And Jade shook her head.

So I obeyed.

I went to her side, knelt, pulled her head to my shoulder as I whispered whatever sweet things an old warrior might think of into her hair. I promised her the River Seine. A life of joy free of corruption. Pretty things.

So many pretty things I had found and hoarded for her to smile at.

Freedom. Even from me should she wish it.

And with those words, she parted her lips and drank of death.

For a third time. For yes, I had watched this woman's every breath for the last agonizing days.

Two painful gulps, and her eyes would never be blue again.

Red as fire, mind deconstructed, she met my gaze, and she saw me for what I was.

Her slave.

25

JADE

I cannot even imagine what my father's body must have gone through when he'd been changed from man to immortal. Once upon a time, a proud Persian king, then the creation of something powerful beyond measure. Did my father even recognize what gifts were given to him in his early state of ignorance? Did he think all vampires were like the man who'd offered him eternity? Had he any idea what Vladislov was?

For I was certain, *Grandfather* was as powerful then as he was now.

Yet in the two interactions I'd witnessed between the men, I had seen no familial conversation. Vladislov had received no more formal a greeting than other emissaries or visiting ancients. There was no closeness, no endearment.

No sense of shared history.

At least none that I understood. Maybe because they were so old. Maybe because my father had no heart. He certainly didn't love his people, neglecting the throne for months at a time, hidden away and secretive.

One day you'd turn around, and Satan would be in the room. Smiling, dressed in glittering robes. Beautiful, devious, and ready to rend. Like clockwork twice a year or so.

Twice a year to mangle my mind, send his hive into a manic uproar, and then leave after ripping apart enough of our numbers to keep the flock in line. I expected little more from my grandfather.

In fact, I expected less.

Considering what he'd just unleashed within me.

I knew what his blood was, and I knew how insignificant this flock was in comparison. Not even an afterthought. But he was drawn to this place, so for that reason alone, he was going to take it. And when he was bored—and he would grow bored—he'd wander on to walk the River Seine, philosophizing about concepts beyond my understanding with God only knew who.

Because really, in comparison to the years I'd just swallowed with a few mouthfuls of his blood, I was still nothing but a fetus.

One that felt extremely strange and very, very

angry now that I felt power for the first time in my horrible life.

So angry, in fact, that it ate up the rest of me, my insecurities and failures burned to ash with the flood of vengeful intention. As if I could shine with the blazing heat of the sun and burn all undead who dared stand so close to something so full of wrath.

From the way Malcom shielded his eyes with a curse, and how the ground shook as he reeled back —how I steamed and rattled, and heard the conservatory's unbreakable, bullet-proof glass crack and fall all around me, it must be so.

Vladislov had once asked me what I would do to the Cathedral had I the power to act as I pleased. And that old wish was taking place without any effort on my part. In fact, I wasn't sure I could stop myself from razing it to the ground.

I lacked any kind of self-control to contain such unimaginable power.

"Remember, young one." Grandfather put his hand to my shoulder, careless of the bright light that had sent Malcom to vanish into the shadows or fry. "No flames. Give half of them a chance to survive, your Marie Antoinette included. Just exorcise the ghosts of this decrepit old place and leave the bones behind."

As if what he commanded were so easy. As if I could stop myself when I felt out the weaknesses of stone and exploited them. Overcharged, inexperienced, and burning from the inside out, I found my body moving from place to place. As if I'd willed it. One moment in the boudoir of one of the cruelest males I'd been forced to take within my body.

All it took was my presence to see his flailing form turned to ash. He'd never even had the chance to scream.

I was the sun. I was death, eating through my people in a very different way than I was infamous for. All the while, those who haunted the Cathedral screamed, scrambling into the night to find cover as stone cracked and entire sections of this ancient, cursed church collapsed into rubble.

How many I killed? I cannot say. And not all were intentional, too many just got in the way as I popped in and out of existence. Ending my massacre in the throne room where my father waited, bloodied from I know not what, and burning with his own power—that was far more immense than mine.

"You ungrateful, useless child!"

There was just enough to his demeanor to see that my sire was rattled, all the more apparent for he'd missed the most important feature of the room.

Immaculate, dressed in a black suit somehow untouched by the dust falling from a building that still shook, Vladislov sat my father's throne.

Witnessed by the many factions who'd fled to this very spot in search of rescue. There was the foreign contingent, stolid and unmoved by the carnage. There were my father's sentinels, others transformed for their beauty or gifts in the arts, the rabble, even the fresh-changed. So many, all who would witness my end.

Already I felt the hand of death, cold, comforting, offering me rest. So I faced it as the daughter of a royal, with my head held high and my words vicious. "You are an unworthy king and a disgrace as a father. I am ashamed to have known you, Darius. And before I die, I will bring this Cathedral down to crush you into dust!"

From me. Those words had come from me. And they were sick with all the things he'd done, the mistakes I'd made, the world that was a worse place because we both existed in it.

"You wouldn't dare!"

"Enough." Vladislov broke through the creak of stone and the roar of my father's anger. "Enough, child."

The valve of unrelenting power the ancient had opened in me closed, stolen away, just as easily as it had been given—simple words from his mouth more powerful than any vendetta I might possess. Just like that, I was the little girl in the blue dress, swinging from her father's arm, recalling child-like joy and the sensation of completeness before my head had been split in half.

That was the perfect way to feel when my father tore my heart out. Whole.

I closed my eyes and braced for it.

Whatever parts of me that had been left in my grandfather's pocket were mine again. I didn't even feel the pain when a red-eyed demon whose features I carried reached forward faster than even the undead could see. The sound of a ribcage cracking, the gagging noise of blood shooting up both windpipe and esophagus, yet it felt like nothing more than a scratch.

This rebirth would be painless.

Or so I thought... until a body slumped against me, taller, larger, and had me tripping over my feet to catch him as he fell. An angel's face contorted in pain, *my angel*, with a gaping hole in his chest and his beating heart in the harsh grip of my father.

Malcom.

"No!" Throwing my body over his, my banshee scream shook the crumbling rafters. Our eyes met, my heart refusing to beat if his wasn't going to exist. And I realized, as his blood bubbled over my fingers, what love felt like.

How I'd felt it for this man from the moment I'd looked up at him as a babe.

How it was terrifying, and fresh, and the most

beautiful thing that might ever exist. And that there was no life worth living if he wasn't in it, bossing me about and challenging me to be better.

I truly was dying, even if my body was whole. "Malcom... no."

In my arms, his glowing eyes were losing their luster. Yet still he tried to smile through the blood, mouthing that he loved me and begging me cast a gate and run.

That would never happen. I'd die here, with him, seeing him as he was: the glowing light of my life in a world that was nothing but dark. And I swore this to him as I kissed his mouth and tasted heaven.

"Poorly done, son." The lightness of the decree from the throne, made my loss seem insignificant.

So it was to him, I begged for Malcom's life. "Eternal fealty if you save him."

With a smile, the ancient turned me down. "No."

Standing, finding my father held the heart of the man meant to me mine, watching him prepare to crush it into jelly and laugh, I struck.

Vladislov barked with the voice of a God, "I said enough!"

Shaken to my soul, caught in midair and dropped to the ground by an unseen power. I gasped for breath and found that Vladislov didn't require eternal fealty from one as puny as me. He only need speak and I was his thrall.

And from where I struggled for breath, when I fought every muscle in my body that refused to move so I might reach the dying heart of my beloved, it seemed my father suffered the same.

The devil himself was frozen solid, clearly fighting the enthrallment and unable to break free.

As my people observed in absolute silence.

With a heavy sigh, Vladislov stood from the throne. Buttoning his suit jacket, an expression of immense disappointment aging his face by eons, he walked down the dais to where his offspring and his grandchild thought to end one another. "Why make her weak when she could be such an asset to our race? Those, Darius, are the actions of an insubstantial man. There is a difference between wielding power and ruling by fear. I have told you this time and time again. The world has no room for creatures like you in these modern times. My child, you have refused to adapt, created a kingdom so flawed that a mere child tore it asunder in one night. I taught you better than that."

My father, vibrating with the power held by a stronger beast, hissed, "You wouldn't dare steal what's mine. Not after all I've given you!"

"The illusion that any of this was ever really yours baffles me the most." Hand to his chest, dignified in a way I'd never witnessed from this changeable man, I fought with every bit of power Vladislov had poured into me to break the compulsion so I might reach that black heart in my father's blood-drenched grip before it ceased to beat.

Inch by inch, my hand stretched forward. But God, the pain, what I had to sacrifice to raise my arm and brush my fingers over my only love's stolen heart. And still I fought the will of an ancient, one who could see me ended with but a thought... prying that heart from my father's fingers.

Because it was mine, and always had been.

Bones broke as I struggled to take a step toward the fallen Malcom. To piece him back together as he had once done for me. Tears streaming down my face, I made it those three agonizing paces, to fall over his body, and find that his eyes were already closed.

"She's very impressive," Grandfather said as he edged nearer to watch.

The heart I put back, pumping it with my hand as veins and arteries reached for their necessary muscle. Slicing my wrist with little claws, I bled for him straight into that gaping hole in his chest. Red blood that had gone several shades closer to black. And I begged Malcom to come back to me.

But he didn't wake up, and that fluttering heart in my hands skipped beats, failing before my eyes.

My sobbing witnessed by so many, the sound of my own heart breaking louder than the crush of tumbling stone, I somehow found the power to stand. Crumpled, as if held together by overstretched tendon and misaligned bones, I crept back to my father, to my grandfather, and I shoved my hand straight into the chest of my lifelong devil, ripping out what lay inside. Because I was owed—so much more than my father's heart—but this was all I'd ever be able to claim from him.

Falling to my knees, I tore out Malcom's ruined organ and put the black heart of pure evil in its place.

It pumped steadily, weaving with tissues and fascia, bring life back to the dead. The man I loved began to mend, lashes parting as if he'd woken from a deep slumber. To hear me say the truest words that had ever passed my lips, "I love you."

26

"Do you hear that, son?" It was gentle, approving, and unnaturally creepy. "She *loves* him."

Shielding Malcom's rapidly healing body with mine, I watched a dance between a wounded cobra and a slinking mongoose. The cobra capable only of waving his head back and forth, the mongoose circling for the kill.

Darius, heartless as he was, wasn't dead.

As our fallen king stood before his kingdom, his maker rent him limb from limb. Only to gently place those severed bits in multiple satin lined, disturbingly-sized caskets, carried forward by Vladislov's contingent.

And I'm sure I was not the only soul in that wreckage of a room who worried that one such as

Darius might never be able to know a true death. Still, I witnessed what would pass for his end. Shivering to see the level of preparation Vladislov had aspired to.

All of this would have taken place no matter my part in it.

They gathered an arm or a leg, quarters of torso, spilled guts. Each container the proper size to hold the piece of the immortal whose heart would beat on forever in the body of another.

In a man who was worthy.

My grandfather's dissection of his son wasn't messy work, considering. Concise, organized, preplanned and ultimately... sad. Darius was dismembered, brought down from greatness as if nothing more than a dandelion puff blown apart by a passing breeze.

And then the boxes holding what had once made up my father were silently carted off by strangers from strange lands with their own unknown agendas. All the while I imagined those bits would be hidden in various parts of the world, burned, buried, maybe left to rot.

Sold to voodoo queens.

But our fallen king's head remained, cupped in the arms of his creator. A head still blinking, a mouth still moving. Alive.

A long span passed, an hour, maybe more, as my

grandfather considered his child. And though his expression failed to alter, I wondered if he felt remorse. But I feared he felt nothing, and that the nothing inside him had somewhat left the ancient surprised.

Imagine growing to such an age where one questioned feeling *anything* at all. Such an existence would be worse than even the life I had lived.

"You don't need to cry for him, Jade." My Malcom, already sitting up as if his ruined heart didn't lie on the floor at his side, stroked my cheek, offering me comfort.

That shriveled heart dead on the ground called to me, that piece of my angel. So I took it. I held it, finding the flesh had gone white as all the blood had drained out.

A shriveled white heart that I would not give up for anything.

Arms came around me, an entirely new sensation. This was a feeling I would grow addicted to. Melting against the greater strength of a man who had given his worthy life for my disgraceful one. Warm tears on a bloodstained face, holding the dead heart of my lover, I found that I did feel enough sorrow for both myself and my grandfather.

There were so many lost moments to mourn.

Had I the true strength, I would have killed

Darius. He deserved to be broken apart, locked in caskets, scattered and forgotten. He deserved hell.

But God didn't work that way. Not for my kind. And watching it happen felt far too real.

"What now?" I wasn't even sure who I'd asked.

Vladislov eyes dragged from the face of his son, finding mine. A moment later he held out his prize. "I believe it's been an age since Darius has seen the sunrise. Be a dear, and take your father for one last look."

Startling us all, he dropped the head, just like that, to crack and bounce on the floor. Fate leaving it to roll my way. And then as if all were forgotten, Vladislov climbed the dais, unbuttoned his jacket, smiling at the chaos of the room as he sat the throne.

Whatever speech he gave my people, whatever was worked, designed, and arranged, I missed. With shaking fingers, I collected Darius by hair as dark as mine. With shaking legs, I did as I was bade.

Malcom did not follow.

After all, he'd pledged eternal fealty and a simple shake of the head from his new king was enough to trap my angel with the rest of the flock.

So off I went. Dazed, drained, wounded, and victorious. I went through the wreckage I'd made with little more than a whim.

At the edge of the fallen debris, I found a crack

in an exterior wall wide enough so I might drag my body from darkness into budding life.

The gardens.

The same gardens I had played in as a child. The gardens I'd looked through from my glass cage. And came to stand before what had once been my conservatory. Now, nothing more than bent metal and razor-sharp shards of glass

Taking this all in, holding dear Daddy's living head by the hair, I had no clue what to do with myself... what to do with him.

I know what he deserved, I grasped what was intended here, but enacting it was...

How?

Perhaps grandfather had felt grief dismantling his child. Perhaps this last step he found he could not do himself. Maybe that's why he stared so long into the pain-filled, fluttering eyes of his creation.

Standing in the field of everything I'd broken, I glanced down at what hung from my arm. What couldn't even look up to see the expression on my face. "I think he did love you, however creatures like him know how to love."

And now there was work to do.

I took a step toward a twisted bit of metal that had once been banked by panes of glass—a piece of my prison—and found it suiting. Like a pike, it rose from the cracked ground, sharp, tall, appropriate for a view of such a lovely garden.

"I loved you too," I said, lifting the head without meeting Daddy's blood-red eyes.

Shoving it upon the spike made the exact sound one might expect a head crammed onto a pike might make. And there Darius would stay, unable to scream, facing the east to take in the sunrise. I'm not sure if it was out of kindness—so that he would not be alone in those final minutes—or if it was out of an unbroken sense of obligation, but I remained at his side as the first rays peeked over the horizon.

He burned at first light, smelling of sulfur and evil, melting onto that metal rod until nothing but a mass of charred flesh and blinding bone showed through the fiery mass. Yet, inside that ruined shell, I was uncertain if he still lived. If day by day he'd suffer over and over in the blazing beauty of sunlight. If that were his punishment for whatever true sin he'd committed against a creature so impossibly more powerful than him, it was laughable.

I didn't know if he'd heal without blood, or for how long he'd be left on display. I didn't know if he'd be stolen by a zealot, or if the birds might eat him. All I knew was that I was reborn in the wafting stink from his smoking flesh.

And that I wasn't going to cry anymore.

That night, I fell asleep in Malcom's arms. I awoke in Malcom's arms. I took sustenance from his body and pleasure from his attention. And as the evenings stretched by, there were no more political events or human maneuverings. No parties or fundraisers or bending over in back alleys for my father's chosen stud.

Instead, there was a world to see, and a loving warrior to guide me through it. Though I'd lived in that city from birth, I knew nothing of it but what I'd been required to experience. So, he took me to restaurants, he took me dancing, played with me, taught me to smile.

Malcom gave me opulent gifts, and poetry in languages I couldn't decipher. He took me out to films. We walked in parks. I learned about him: the names of his mother and sisters, the battles he'd fought and triumphs he still recalled with pride. His favorite color and the blood type he preferred above all others.

And though I was still uncomfortable with the change, the man took great pride in the fact that my eyes were now the same shade as the ruby he'd locked around my throat. A trait that made it a touch harder for me to fit in with humans, but was easily concealed with contacts or chic sunglasses.

Malcom taught me how to hunt, just as he would have taught any freshly-turned. He gave me access to his herd, and I found their existence not near as dreary as I'd imagined. The blood of happy humans was so much sweeter than that of those who despaired, he'd said. Not that my angel was a saint. He was a carnivore, the ultimate predator, and I found watching him feed to be exceedingly erotic.

And though I had no desire to mingle with them, I began to understand my people. A people vastly reduced in this part of the world. Less than half of what had been left within the throne room when I'd left survived that night. Vladislov had scores to settle. I'd even heard a rumor that he'd approached the former queen of France, smiling as he'd told her that sharing that cake with me decades ago was the only reason any had been left alive at all. Marie Antoinette had not found the 'let them eat cake' reference anything but terrifying. Which Vladislov, no doubt, found hilarious.

I wished never to go back there. Should those survivors wish to see me, they would come to my building, my kingdom, my sanctuary where Malcom saw to my every last need… almost.

"When?" I demanded, impatient in every way.

Smiling, nuzzling my neck, Malcom murmured, "Soon."

Through those days and those nights and those moments with my lover, I had known deep gratification and a lightness of spirit, but I had also known deprivation. Though he would give me endless physical pleasure, he had denied me his cock.

And made me a beggar.

For weeks. Months. Seasons.

Don't get me wrong, his fingers and tongue were magic. The tricks he knew beyond imagining. The man was capable of getting me worked up into such a state I sang out his name like a hymn. But that cock, unless I was feeding from one of its veins, it was not in my mouth or my pussy.

He called me his virgin.

I found I relished the endearment far more than I should.

"Define soon!" Because this was torture, this endless waiting with no real answer. I was so wet, always wet, and I had not forgotten the feel of him. Which is why I primarily chose to dine from the prominent vein twisting up the side of a glorious erection. It was the only way to tempt him to spill. To let his seed mingle with his blood and leave me boneless yet sadly empty.

"No."

"Am I being punished?"

Another of his grins, freely given and so beautiful I sometimes forgot what I meant to say. "You are being adored."

Diving between my legs, he licked my clit with abandon, rough with a flick of his tongue at the end of each swipe until my legs shook, and I found I'd lost the words to beg for more. Replete and breathless, I'd lain like a bit of flotsam on the waves, and felt him snuggle me.

"When I claim you—savagely fuck you, as you so elegantly demand—you'll never doubt what you are to me. I'll know when you're ready, and that day is not today."

Bastard! He didn't get to dictate or deny me something I'd had practically every single day of my existence. Something it would seem I could hardly think straight without.

A single time I'd threatened to find another who would ride me until I was satisfied.

I saw real anger that night. I felt it in the sting on my skin when I'd been pulled over his knee.

That same night he'd given me Ethan, freshly-changed and ridiculous. Arrogant, and unaware that he was trapped in servitude for a century or more. Though this had been explained to him repeatedly before Malcom found him ready to enter our home.

Which Ethan still considered *his* home.

He went straight to the fridge to grab a beer,

popping off the cap and taking a swig, only to immediately spit it back up. There would be no more craft brews in his future, a concept that had still failed to sink in.

That entitlement alone made him unattractive to me, though vampirism had done nothing but add to his beauty. He'd kissed me. The taste of his mouth on mine when he'd rushed forward with all the enthusiasm of a puppy, was unwelcome.

Malcom had given me his word. My body for this creature. Our agreement was that I could fuck Ethan to handle my urges. And Ethan was hard, very hard, as he rubbed against me and rambled on about all the clubs we'd be seen at together. How as immortals we'd control Wall Street, the White House, rule the city like king and queen.

"And what of your blonde and your child?"

Did he not realize he'd never see either of them again? That he'd not be permitted in public for at least two generations?

He acted as if nothing had been mentioned.

After all, he'd learned I was a princess. I could pull strings and there was no need for him to serve. Maybe I'd give him a sip of my blood so he could go into the sun too! Oh, we'd go to Belize, soak up the rays and play in the waves.

This man was an idiot.

And though I was practically starving for cock, his was the last I'd consider.

Malcom had taken him away. I think he might have killed him afterward, to be honest. I didn't care; I just never wanted to see him again.

The whole event had left me in a mood for a night or two, one lifted by a trip to the opera with a beautiful man on my arm. And a sea of familiar faces unsure why I ignored their invitations and waved them away from my box.

I wore white. I always wore white for Malcom, and I suspected that had I placed a veil on my head, it would have done nothing but given my vampire pleasure.

And it hit me, leaving me smiling during intermission as if I were in on his trick. "You're waiting for me to call you my husband."

Malcom kissed my fingers and said nothing.

The lights flickered, and the second act began.

27

MALCOM

It took her a year. Pouting, arguments. Four seasons, timed almost to the day that she'd brought down the Cathedral to begin truly accepting her place in my world. One year for her to be ready, to experience a healthy relationship and life the way a *modern* immortal might crave.

We had all the time in the world for her to capitulate. But she would not be truly happy without that one last, small concession. Patience I could and would afford her. Not that she wasn't regularly corrected. Over my knee, with orgasm denial, with timeouts and physical restraint. Still so young, so impetuous, so *mine*.

I didn't ask when I'd thrown out all the clothing she'd owned before she'd become my wife. My female—my pure, clean, worthy female—would wear white, and only white. Let her believe it was she who chose such things to please me. Let her scoff when a true wedding gown, carefully selected of course, came to hang in a position of obvious importance in her closet.

The minx refused to call me husband.

Were I introduced to humans at all, it was only as Malcom. Even if I pawed her before other interested men. Even if I kissed her dizzy and smeared all that red lipstick she loved to paint on her mouth.

She found my silent insistence on the term irrelevant. Thought to punish me for refusing her my cock, though she was blood and cum drunk on me several times a day. Absolutely addicted. Those glowing red eyes of hers never even glanced in the direction of another male or female. Quite a feat, considering her appetites and former temperament.

The collar locked around her throat, she could not get it off. This bothered her greatly. But the statement it made was far more important than her frustration. We were *forever*. A concept for one so young that had to feel weighty and intimidating.

I might never remove that collar from her throat, what care had I if it clashed with her fashion choices or *chafed* her skin. One day as a God, she'd still wear it.

"You don't wear a collar! You don't wear a ring!" This she'd spat at me when I'd caught her at her vanity picking at the mechanism with some tool. A tool she'd thrown with such precision it had pierced me right through the shoulder. Which was fucking hot as hell. My princess was learning.

An hour later there was a ring on my finger. I'd been keeping it on hand for just this occasion.

At first glance of the hammered band of steel, she blushed, frustrated to be thwarted, then settled into my side so I might read to her in old languages. So she might know she was safe, loved, and would endure through her tricky transition.

Jade healed.

Considering the amounts of blood she'd swallowed straight from a demon's veins, it still took a remarkable amount of time. I'd catch her in the kitchen, talking to herself as she made a sandwich, piecing out old memories and not sure which was real and which was fake. She'd get stuck in circular arguments with her reflection, grow frustrated to the point of tears, drain me, as if the answers might lie at the center of my steadily beating heart… if only she could get to it.

What mattered most was that *she* had made herself the sandwich. It sounded like so small a thing, but was so epic in a world where she had hardly wiped her own ass.

So we would talk and I would tell her what I knew, fact from fiction. What I could not confirm, we'd consider together. And I found in doing this, I too began remembering things. Things that had Darius still ruled, he would have crushed me on the spot for holding in memory.

Devious Darius had a great secret.

One he'd gone to remarkable lengths to conceal.

With part of him alive in me, there was just enough to recall *her* face. I'd torn out *her* fangs and delivered *her* to a rotting, bored, and unkind king who had not moved from his throne in a century—not even to feed.

One who from that day forward no longer sat his throne.

One who abandoned us all for... a Pearl.

Jade

The evil had not been exorcised, but it had been *shifted* just enough to make it tolerable. Unsure if that was the proper description, I ignored the sounds of construction, ignored that simply approaching the passageway to such a place made me sick to my stomach. And I entered the Cathedral, though I'd sworn to myself I'd never do so again.

A new freshly-turned servant waited, and unlike the previous history of flagging, stupid, rude, and wasted baby vamps, this one knew me by sight. "My lady."

To the pretty girl I turned over a snow-white coat, my pair of crystal-encrusted Louboutins clicking over fresh marble floors when I walked past. Marveling. The whole vestibule for my favored entrance had been redone, the center table boasting a massive spray of fresh flowers highlighted by *electric light*.

Unnerving.

The massive, spiked wooden door between this false façade and the altar to the undead throne had somehow survived my onslaught, rehung and waiting, should I dare push it open.

It wouldn't do to be seen hesitating before a servant, yet still my hand met the wood and I failed to push.

"He's expecting you." Kindly offered, extremely nervous, she tapped a message into her tablet.

The *he* in question had not been told I'd been coming. Not even Malcom knew I was here. But Vladislov was a veritable God. And only Gods knew what Gods could see.

Hinges sang, well-oiled as I bore my weight against something it would take ten mortal men to move. And then I was home.

The Cathedral.

I might have thought I was Alice stepping through the looking glass, this world so different, far removed from the one I'd known.

Yet almost the same.

Stone, candelabras, the scent of beeswax and incense and oil. But bright with electric light. Under my radically expensive shoes some cracked stones remained, highlighted by new, fresh blocks of rock. As if the building itself was testament to what had happened here. And what could happen again. The walls were... changed? They were the same? Mirrors and paintings—a painting of me wearing white—and tapestries and literal cave drawings all brought in to highlight a throne that my father had sat.

Had ruined.

That had been taken from him on a whim.

And that sat empty.

He was waiting for me, the girl had said. But he was not here.

How I had suffered in this room once upon a time. Not just the day my brains had been dashed against a wall, but for decades afterward when I had been brought low and shamed. And that throne sat empty.

And *he* failed to appear.

So I dared.

Much.

I dared my life to climb the steps of the dais as I had as a child, to put my hands to the armrests I'd swung from all those ages ago. And I sat my ass in that seat.

Head steeped in my hands, exhausted from the work of it, I found a minuscule slice of rest in my exploit. This wasn't play. I wasn't queen. I'd never rule, and I hated most of the survivors who'd been forced to rebuild what I'd demolished.

"It suits you."

I didn't look up, not with my head spinning as it was, but I did answer my grandfather. "Coming here was a mistake."

Footfalls I heard as he climbed the steps. "One of many you will make, and learn from. Mistakes define what we are. Each worth so much more than any victory."

Was that so? Well then, I was rich in experience and saccharine in the smile I offered. I couldn't put my finger on why, but I was angry with this man. *This thing* who'd hung my picture on the wall. This force that had upset my life and left me with glowing red eyes. "I don't know what to do."

"Well… I'm so unaccustomed to honesty when it comes to our kind where do I even begin to answer?" The teasing, it was so Vladislov.

Sagging back, boneless and finding the seat

infinitely uncomfortable, I snarked, "My guess would be that you demand I stand from your throne. Perhaps you tear off a limb or two, drive home the point that this was no place for Darius's whore daughter to rest."

It was always that waved brown hair I noticed first. Perfect in the unison of its movement. Then it was the ugliness of his beautiful voice. "But you currently sit the throne. Should it not be you who command me?"

I'd play this game. "I command you to release Malcom from his vow."

"Done! See how easy it is to rule as queen?"

He had to be joking! Had to be. For if he wasn't, I might bring down this entire new building and piss on the ashes. But the bastard was adjusting his cufflinks and so goddamn full of himself he may as well have burst from his seams.

I had a life to spend with Malcom and it did not include listening to the bitching of immortals. "No."

And all playfulness was lost in that instant, a demon spreading proverbial wings, that had they existed would span the room in pure flame. Towering over me as I sat his throne, to correct one who dared disagree. It didn't affect me as it would have a year prior. Instead it drew me to my feet to face this thing. This true immortal monster.

"I don't want to be queen."

"At no time did I ask you. Consider that, granddaughter." He pushed a lock of hair behind my ear, reverent in the way he touched my face. "I never ask. Remember that should we banter as the eons pass."

"You promised me the Seine..." And with that latent conversation I should not have held so close to my heart, I'd thought I'd been offered freedom.

"The Seine you shall have, and your husband I shall make free, if..." He, the most powerful vampire that might exist rolled up his sleeve to show me a wrist marked with black veins. "If you drink all your belly can hold."

Just because I was tired of being quashed, because I felt like being a dick and was bored of politics, games, and a life I had no control over, I took my grandfather's wrist. But only to pull him closer so I might go for the throat. Suit jacket pulled aside, I sank in my fangs so the wool might remain unblemished. The same could not be said for the crisp, white undershirt he wore like a Fortune 500 executive. It would be stained. Others would see that someone had fed from Vladislov as if he were food and not ambrosia.

I'd expected my brains to be dashed against the wall for such gall. I'd anticipated pain. *I'd known better!*

But he was far more clever than I. One mouthful

and I saw eternity. A single gulp and I was forever changed. Horrified. Blessed. Unworthy. Pure.

As I drank, a God whispered in my ear, "You don't have to live your life without love. Have your Pict. Take him from me. But you can only keep him if you take this throne. Otherwise, I'll exercise my right to send him where you'll never find him no matter how long you search."

I couldn't imagine surviving a single night without Malcom. So I took the ugly deal, already feeling the building shake around me from my growing temper.

And then Malcom was there, hand to my shoulder, sweet words at my ear. Foundations stopped their rumbling. My heart beat again… full of ichor and swampy darkness that left my eyes an even brighter crimson.

Drawing my teeth from the throat of an eternal, terrible thing, I buried my face in the shirt of my husband.

And married him that night beside the River Seine.

The gown fit to perfection.

The veil made me feel new.

Our bloodthirsty kiss after vows spun by some random priest sent the terrified mortal running back to his church.

Few were invited, yet many arrived. With little

notice, the new Queen of the Americas' wedding became an event for those with rank enough to dare show their face. But there was one there who troubled me. A woman, overwhelmed in appearance, who clung to my grandfather like a tick.

She had dark hair. Blue eyes an exceedingly familiar shade that had once been mine. And stared at me with a mix of awe and horror.

She refused the passed goblets of the finest vintage of human blood. And my grandfather cooed over her, her awkwardness, her impropriety. Her total lack of manners.

My dress was lace, it was white. But my feelings toward that creature were black.

Though I was given no time to explore them. One moment we were before a crowd of undead playing at ceremony, the next I was with my husband in a room so laden with rose petals it was cliché.

Cliché and adorable.

"Tell me you love me." There would be no absolution should I answer incorrectly.

God, how I adored when he commanded me so. "I love you, Maelchon of the Pict."

"You might be queen, but know that I am your king."

He was, so much so that just to hear him speak in that tone had my pussy dripping with need. "I have no king, no husband as yet. Not until you give me what you've denied my body for so long."

And I was speared with such recklessness, that it broke our bed on a single thrust. In that moment, I think I died.

He fucked me raw, over days and nights in a windowless room. Took more than I might give until he filled me with child.

And I came so hard, I swore allegiance to my slave. Gave him my very soul. Felt each thrust of his cock so deeply that I swear it changed my spirit into something new.

A virgin. A husband.

Too rough, biting and vicious, and everything I might ever want.

Utterly in love, ruined by it, I took that throne as Malcom directed the rebuilding of my Cathedral, belly swollen with our firstborn. Who kicked like a fiend.

I was not a biddable queen. I was not amenable. I reordered with violence yet could be gentle as a lamb. Marie brought me cake. To her, I offered grace.

Eventually friendship, even with her despicable mate, Gustavo.

Hating that throne, I kept to my husband, his council, and his attention. He lavished me with far more than wisdom and pleasure.

Malcom made me new. Made all of it bearable.

Until it began to fit. And the Cathedral began to glow with more than electric light.

Internal peace, a thing my people had been starved for.

I gave birth on a Sunday, in the beautiful room Malcom had designed for me. We named our daughter Eithne—Pict for princess. Our ruby. Her eyes a far brighter red than mine.

And as her father slept, I took her out to see the sun.

Thank you for reading CATHEDRAL! Ready to #FreePearl? Vladislov and Pearl's romance awaits! Please enjoy an extended excerpt of THE RELIC...

THE RELIC
Cradle of Darkness, Book Two

Vladislov

All thrones, all palaces, all places in this world where creatures of the night lingered—every corner of every continent where hunting grounds might exist—all of it bored me. I couldn't even recall what state the world had been in, the borders of countries, the wars fought, when I'd last sat as king. Others were placed to carry out that work in my stead. To lord over the night's denizens and keep our kind in line.

Keep my children thriving, learning, adapting, bringing pride to our race.

Darius had been my favorite son, hand-plucked from the Persian court. So much potential… and the ultimate disappointment. Thousands of years were no excuse to forget one's duty and where one came from. Namely from me, who'd chosen him, raised him, taught him, granted him power far beyond what others of our kind possessed.

Power that was abused.

How soon they forget.

So there I sat, on my dismembered son's throne, aghast to be reorganizing a disrupted hive full of

Darius' more evil creations. Their minds were... fascinating. Their inability to answer my questions, clever. My son truly believed his gifts set him on equal footing with his creator. Yet all he did was make a mess. What I was seeing was little more than his extreme selfishness, even for our kind.

There were secrets buried here, in tunnels that spanned the entirety of this city. Thousands of humans trafficked and kenneled, disposed of with none the wiser. That, I would give my boy, was clever. Vampires weren't even a myth in the new world. They were fodder for television shows and movies. Yet thousands lived in this city, hunting, breeding, bickering, and surviving right under the noses of millions of humans.

The evolution of my kind had been curious to observe. From vicious night predators who'd ransack entire towns in one moonlit night, to subtle and stealthy, *wiser*, monsters.

Yet, still a bother. Even with all their new rules and new technology and endless opportunities, some just didn't deserve the gifts they were given. And some were not given enough.

Such as my descendent, Jade. Daughter of my dismembered son Darius with so many remarkable talents for our kind, all stripped from her by dear old dad until she was weaker than the lowliest servant. Until her mind was broken, scarred, and required more blood from my veins than, in my long, long history, I had ever given another.

A soft spot I had for my grandchild, though I imagined in ten thousand years, I'd be dismembering her too.

The beautiful imp looked every bit her father's daughter, no denying the resemblance. But only the fates could say what time and power would make of her. Darius was not the first of my creations I'd been forced to *handle*.

He would not be the last.

A flutter. A single unusual heartbeat at that thought.

I'd rather not see Jade fragmented physically. Not after she'd already been so fragmented mentally. I'd see her rise.

Yet now she played house with her strict lover. Now she recovered, her people recovered, the throne recovered, because I sat a throne for the first time since humans traveled over oceans.

Listening to petty squabbles, culling an overripe herd. Being gracious to my grandchild while simultaneously contemplating war—a mass extinction across all vampire civilizations. The rapture.

Kings and queens all over the world were failing in their rule, chasing pleasure and forgetting to parent. Tithes became poorer, greed was on the rise.

Which could be partially blamed on modern

times, and the infection of selfishness that reigned in all society, human and vampire.

Perhaps a World War was just the thing? Set back this mania, remind all life that death hovered and whispered in their ear.

Without great loss and suffering, what was there to remember to treasure?

Shiny objects? Bit coin? Art?

The only art I admired these days was the portrait of my granddaughter. Painted myself, and perfect. Life-size, dominating the throne room. A testament of millennia of practice with a brush and the old way of mixing oil paints.

A reminder to the few I had let live of just where their allegiance best rest. The first who had scoffed at it, I ripped in half. Careful that none of their blood might mark the canvas. Purposefully drenching all in the room with bits of dead vampire juice.

Baptized in the blood of a fool. Their one and only warning that she was held in my esteem.

I would have preferred to start fresh with this entire court. Donate some of my own dear flock, augment it with new blood. Find young prodigies with modern tendencies and acumen. But darling Jade had been given the option to choose the fate of this flock. So, I left her a few hundred. Though, to be true, in a year or two I might return and kill them

THE RELIC

all if I found myself displeased with how things had progressed. Once I deemed her recovery sufficient and forced her to take the throne.

And I would come back, I always came back to this Cathedral, and had every year for near a century. I'd thought it was my son that drew me, that his inevitable end whispered in my ear. But now he was gone from this place in all the ways that mattered. Yet still I heard the call.

Which made sitting a throne a bit more bearable.

"My lord."

Ah yes, the one who loved my grandchild. Shining head bowed, manners impeccable, I found I liked Malcom... a very little. "What has she done now?"

These tales were always amusing. His weekly reports while she slept something I looked forward to in this endless slog on the chair.

"She is... perfect." Rushing through his speech on her recent accomplishments, shaking his head, the man changed topics. Clearly nervous. "I didn't come here to discuss Jade. There is something... I remembered."

It was unlike this one to trip on his words. Which widened my eyes in anticipation, and left me leaning forward, fingers steepled and smirk on my mouth.

"Something"—glowing eyes met mine, concern,

a touch of fear as if he might not leave this conversation with the borrowed heart in his chest—"that I must show you."

I smiled broadly, standing from the throne, amused by something different. *Anything* different. "By all means. Lead the way."

Long ago, blocked off and forgotten, this area of the Cathedral should not exist. Not on any schematics, not in the memories of those left alive here or stumbled upon in their excavations. But there it was, hidden behind so many layers of random, unused rooms, barred doors, spiraling ancient stairways so tight one had to bend in half just to navigate the descent.

Any recollection of this place had been ripped as violently as Darius might from every last mind who had ever known of it. There weren't even rats, so tightly it had been sealed. Only damp, and cobwebs, and an utter lack of light.

Even eyes like mine could hardly see in this type of dark.

And I found I loved it. The vibration of the walls, the desolation.

It was a prison, once the burial chambers of the clergy this ground had been stolen from. Cells with iron bars where the dead inside had long ago gone to bone, or desiccated to the point a strong wind would blow them apart like paper.

Other cells had been fully bricked over, whoever left inside trapped for eternity, and I had a strong suspicion I might know a few missing vampires of a certain age who, by chance, might grace a cell or two.

And had no interest in relieving them from their box.

Not when I heard something I might only describe as singing, not when I felt drawn forward through that nightmare. Following the siren song, I became impatient of the debris, crushing what I might, tossing it haphazardly behind me for Malcom to dodge.

I moved without his direction straight to a wall where the bricks didn't match and the mortar was sloppy and thick.

And knocked three times for good measure.

At my back, Malcom confessed. "I put her in here. Ordered the masons to brick it shut... and forgot that very night I'd ever laid eyes on the waif. *Everyone forgot.* This whole area just... disappeared."

Ah. Perhaps dear Malcom was worthy of my granddaughter after all.

As if to soften what he thought to be a disappointing blow, the male muttered, "There is no guarantee she's still inside. He could have taken her anywhere…"

Oh, but Darius had not. Not if he'd gone to such trouble to have something so unusual right under my nose. "I can hear her, singing an old tune. Not asleep and not awake."

And ready to be uncovered. Brick… something as inconsequential as brick was all he'd needed to cage a true daywalker. Breaking through the mortar with black extended claws, pulling apart a wall that whined with the removal of each stone, the whole slab having settled and grown accustomed to its missing support, I found a door like any other prison door. Unremarkable and built to make the prisoner know they were there to suffer.

Moments later, that wood was dust, fragments crumbling, with little more than a swipe of my hand. And on the other side? The back of a massive gilded, gaudy, ornate, and hideous mirror. A huge monstrosity of a mirror that completely covered where the door had been.

Tempted to break it, so eager was I to enter, I held back the urge and slid it gently to the side.

To feast my eyes upon a prison cell transformed.

Darius... so predictable. So petty.

To keep this from me! Here.

Underground with the rot. To know what he had wasn't his. To have dared lied about the origin of his child!

He and I would have words about this. Most especially to think that all his golden candelabras and expensive furnishings were good enough for what had been trapped inside. The crypt still stank of blood and sex and tears and longing. Priceless paintings gone to mold in the dank, Persian rug half eaten by fungus and mold.

Four poster bed, dressed in tatters. Red rags splattered black from old dried blood that still smelled of sunlight, even down here.

Jewels, treasures, secrets.

A room for pleasure derived from pain.

This was a place in which Malcom was entirely unwelcome, and I cast him back before he might set his eyes to the lovely corpse on the bed. "Leave us. Return to your bride, for her time of rest is almost at an end."

"My lord." Retreating into the dark, he moved with superhuman speed, as if aware how utterly possessive I was of this uncovered treasure. And how tempted I was to kill him just for standing too near.

Pity I had not chosen finer garments for this

moment. That I had not brought gifts. My beloved had always loved flowers. Beautiful horses. The scent of pine.

"Here you are, as gorgeous as I remember," I murmured to her withered skull, gently placing my hip to the bed so her remains might not be disturbed. "How long I've waited. So many centuries searching."

Smoothing back hair that fell from her skull, I leaned over my darling one. "What it means to me to know you kept your promise…" Overfull with a sensation I'd almost completely forgotten, my voice shook. "You swore to me you'd be reborn. Sleeping, waiting for me to find you."

Under my nose for a century. Here where she could have been crushed and lost again while I'd let Jade wreak havoc on the building.

My own displeasure was shaking the foundations as it was. Setting a rainfall of dust motes to cloud the room. Leaning over to kiss her mouth. Or where her lips would have been had they not shriveled back over her teeth, I tried so very hard to be gentle. "Tell me you knew I'd come?"

The corpse, eyes long ago shriveled, said nothing. Failed to move. Failed to do anything but lie on a bed stained with her blood. My poor beloved had been alone since Darius had been dismembered, and from the state of the room, alone and suffering.

Perhaps I would go into the garden later and have more than a talk with the head on a pike. Perhaps if the smells under the rot of this place were any sign of what he'd done to her, I'd crush that skull to jelly and eat it.

Blind, my love was. Her hearing, the eardrums, I suspected might be intact enough that she at least heard the cadence of my song to her. That she knew I was here, would never allow her from my sight again.

The nubs of her fangs far too short for the work of slicing through my flesh were inconsequential. My true worry was that any attempt to part her jaw might break it, desiccated as it was.

Problem easily solved. I kissed her mouth again, and sliced my wrist with a quick flick of a black claw. "Drink and wake. Come back to me."

My blood was poison, laced with nature's contempt for our kind. Yet it contained eternal, monotonous, never-changing life. Pouring it down a throat that could not swallow, I sat with her for the endless hour it took to reinvigorate her, cell by cell.

Nothing was more glorious than seeing my gifts reconstitute lovely blue eyes.

They had been blue in her last life too.

Her daughter's had been that very shade before I'd changed her into something more. A clue I should have recognized had I paid more attention to the fact Darius kept my grandchild from my sight.

She took a breath, that rattled her half-reformed ribcage. There was pain in those sky-blue eyes.

A flush to cheeks that were fair and high. Dark hair, long and luxurious.

She drank every drop I might squeeze from my veins, swallowed as I gathered her close.

And was so very afraid of me.

That wouldn't do. So, ever the charmer, I spun our tale. Starting at the beginning—this new beginning. "Your name in this life is Pearl. Mine these days is Vladislov. And I have been looking for you for an eternity."

Read THE RELIC now!

ADDISON CAIN

USA TODAY bestselling author and Amazon Top 25 bestselling author, Addison Cain's dark romance and smoldering paranormal suspense will leave you breathless.
Obsessed antiheroes, heroines who stand fierce, heart-wrenching forbidden love, and a hint of violence in a kiss awaits.

For the most current list of exciting titles by Addison Cain, please visit her website: addisoncain.com

- facebook.com/AddisonlCain
- bookbub.com/authors/addison-cain
- goodreads.com/AddisonCain

ALSO BY ADDISON CAIN

Don't miss these exciting titles by Addison Cain!

Standalone:

Swallow it Down

Strangeways

The Golden Line

The Alpha's Claim Series:

Born to be Bound

Born To Be Broken

Reborn

Stolen

Corrupted

Wren's Song Series:

Branded

Silenced

The Irdesi Empire Series:

Sigil

Sovereign

Que (coming soon)

Cradle of Darkness Series:

Catacombs

Cathedral

The Relic

A Trick of the Light Duet:

A Taste of Shine

A Shot in the Dark

Historical Romance:

Dark Side of the Sun

Horror:

The White Queen

Immaculate

CPSIA information can be obtained
at www.ICGtesting.com
Printed in the USA
LVHW112153081022
730275LV00025B/296